Seeing Eye

Seeing Eye

S T O R I E S

Michael Martone

𝒵

ZOLAND BOOKS

Cambridge, Massachusetts

First edition published in 1995 by
Zoland Books, Inc.
384 Huron Avenue
Cambridge, Massachusetts 02138

Copyright © 1995 by Michael Martone

FIRST EDITION

Book design by Boskydell Studio

Printed in the United States of America

Ths book is printed on acid-free paper, and its binding
materials have been chosen for strength and durability.

Library of Congress Cataloging-in-Publication Data
Martone, Michael.
Seeing eye : stories / Michael Martone. — 1st ed.
p.   cm.
ISBN 0-944072-51-8 (acid free paper)
I. Title.
PS3563.A7414S4   1995
813'.54 — dc20   95-22744
CIP

For John Barth and Monroe Engel
and in memory of
Margaret Wiggs, Richard Cassell, and James Lewinski,
my teachers

ACKNOWLEDGMENTS

The author wishes to thank the editors of the following magazines and presses for their support and for their permission to reprint these stories here. "The Mayor of the Sister City Talks to the Chamber of Commerce in Klamath Falls, Oregon," in *Sundog*. "Dish Night," "Meat," "What I See," "The Teakwood Deck of the USS *Indiana*," "Limited," and "Highlights" in *Indiana Review*. "Lice" and "Fidel" in *The Florida Review*. "Three Tales of the Sister City" in *Telescope*. "Guam," "Blue Hair," and "Turning the *Constellation*" in *Colorado Review*. "The War That Never Ends" in *High Plains Literary Review*. "Chatty Cathy Falls into the Wrong Hands" in *The Laurel Review*. "Evaporation" in *Sycamore Review*. "Miners" in *Aura*. "Elkhart, There, at the End of the World" in *Indiana Writes*. "On the Highway of Vice Presidents," "On the Tomb of the Unknown Soldier," "On Anesthesia," "On *The Little Prince*," and "On Snipe Hunting" in *Exquisite Corpse*. "On Snipe Hunting" also appeared in *Harper's*. "On the State of the Union," "On Late-Night TV," and "On Barbie" in *Story*. "On 911" and "On *Quayleito*" in *The Iowa Review*. "It's Time" in *The North American Review*. "Seeing Eye" in *The Arts Indiana Literary Supplement*. "Outside Peru" in *Epoch*. "*Pensées:* The Thoughts of Dan Quayle" appeared as a chapbook published by Broad Ripple Press. "The Teakwood Deck of the USS *Indiana*," "On the State of the Union," "On Hoosier Hysteria," "On *Planet of the Apes*," and "Fidel" also appeared in different versions in *Fort Wayne Is Seventh on Hitler's*

List, published by Indiana University Press. "It's Time" was included in *Voices Louder Than Words,* edited by William Shore, published by Vintage Books. "Seeing Eye" was included in *The Company of Dogs,* edited by Michael J. Rosen, published by Doubleday.

The author also wishes to thank Michael Rosen, Susan Neville, Joseph Trimmer, Chris Leland and Osvaldo Sabino, Susan Dodd, Nancy Esposito, David Rivard and Michaela Sullivan, and, of course, Sallie Gouverneur.

And a generous grant for the completion of this book was provided by Theresa Pappas. "Diastema, we fit together."

CONTENTS

The War
That Never Ends

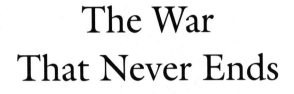

The Mayor of the Sister City Talks
to the Chamber of Commerce
in Klamath Falls, Oregon

"It was after the raid on Tokyo. We children were told to collect scraps of cloth. Anything we could find. We picked over
the countryside; we stripped the scarecrows. I remember this
remnant from my sister's obi. Red silk suns bounced like
balls. And these patches were quilted together by the women
in the prefecture. The seams were waxed as if to make the
stitches rainproof. Instead they held air, gases, and the rags
billowed out into balloons, the heavy heads of chrysanthe-
mums. The balloons bobbed as the soldiers attached the
bombs. And then they rose up to the high wind, so many,
like planets, heading into the rising sun and America. . . ."

I had stopped translating before he reached this point. I
let his words fly away. It was a luncheon meeting. I looked
down at the tables. The white napkins looked like mountain
peaks of a range hung with clouds. We were high above
them on the stage. I am *yonsei,* the fourth American genera-

tion. Four is an unlucky number in Japan. The old man, the mayor, was trying to say that the world was knit together with threads we could not see, that the wind was a bridge between people. It was a hot day. I told these beat businessmen about children long ago releasing the bright balloons, how they disappeared ages and ages ago. And all of them looked up as if to catch the first sight of the balloons returning to earth, a bright scrap of joy.

Dish Night

Every Wednesday was Dish Night at the Wells Theatre. And it worked because she was there, week in and week out. She sat through the movie to get her white bone china. A saucer. A cup. The ushers stood on chairs by the doors and reached into the big wooden crates. There was straw all over the floor of the lobby and bales of newspaper from strange cities. I knew she was the girl for me. I'd walk her home. She'd hug the dish to her chest. The streetlights would be on and the moon behind the trees. She'd talk about collecting enough pieces for our family of eight. "Oh, it's everyday and I know it," she'd say, holding it at arm's length. "They're so modern and simple and something we'll have a long time after we forget about the movies."

I forget just what happened then. She heard about Pearl Harbor at a Sunday matinee. They stopped the movie, and a man came out onstage. The blue stage lights flooded the gold curtain. It was dark in there, but outside it was bright and cold. They didn't finish the show. Business would pick up then, and the Wells Theatre wouldn't need a Dish Night to bring the people in. The one we had gone to the week before was the last one ever and we hadn't known it. The gravy boat looked like a slipper. I went to the war, to Europe, where she'd write to me on lined school paper and never fail to mention we were a few pieces shy of the full set.

This would be the movie of my life, this walking home under the moon from a movie with a girl holding a dinner plate under her arm like a book. I believed this is what I was fighting for. Everywhere in Europe I saw broken pieces of crockery. In the farmhouses, the cafes. Along the roads were drifts of smashed china. On a beach, in the sand where I was crawling, I found a bit of it the sea washed in, all smooth with blue veins of a pattern.

I came home and washed the dishes every night, and she stacked them away, bowls nesting on bowls as if we were moving the next day.

The green field is covered with these tables. The sky is huge and spread with clouds. The pickup trucks and wagons are backed in close to each table so that people can sit on the lowered tailgates. On the tables are thousands of dishes. She walks ahead of me. Picks up a cup then sets it down again. A plate. She runs her finger around a rim. The green field rises slightly as we walk, all the places set at the tables. She hopes she will find someone else who saw the movies she saw on Dish Night. The theater was filled with people. I was there. We do this every Sunday after church.

Lice

I was waiting for the girls to come out of their mother's trailer so I decided to check the tires with a penny I found on the passenger seat. On the left front, the tread wasn't deep enough to reach Lincoln's nose and I could see all the rest were more or less bald. That's when the girls blew out the trailer door. Their coats were half on and half off. It looked like they had a couple of extra arms each, their hair flying.

I stood up and threw the penny away. As soon as I did it I felt sorry. I wanted the penny back right away and looked for it in the tall brown grass. I looked away from the trailer out into the yard, which was turning all copper as the sun went down. I'd never find it.

It was almost winter again. Straw bales were stuffed around the trailer, hiding the wheels and the hitch. The propane tank was newly painted silver. They paint metal silver. That penny was still somewhere in the grass. The girls were pulling each other's hair, and I felt the car sink with the weight of them. I felt it sink under my butt where I leaned on the fender and looked over the cornfield newly gleaned next to where the trailer was parked.

"Daddy," the kids said, "look at us."

My car is silver. The seats are black. The girls were in the nest of their things in back. Paper, rope, arms from old dolls, clothes, books with gold spines, and bent-up plastic straws. They were already reading.

Their mother followed them out this time. She showed me the paper from the school. She hadn't read the note until I'd pulled up in the drive when she was getting the girls' things together. She checked their hair right there while they wormed around in their coats by the door. She combed through the fine hairs behind their ears and in the scruff of their necks and found the ropes of eggs leading down to the scalps and there the lice.

And I stood there a second with her. I thought about the time I let one die overnight on a piece of notebook paper. It clung for hours to a loose hair I put beside it like the grass the girls throw in with lightning bugs. I wanted to see if it was true about needing warm bodies to survive. It was true. And I blew the paper clean.

"We took a nap," she said. And it took me a while to understand what she meant. We were both leaning on the car. She had her head hanging down. Her arms were straight and her hands were jammed into her sweater pockets. I felt my fingers on her scalp, and I leaned in toward the whirlpool of her hair.

Meat

Because I could play baseball, I never went to Korea. I was standing on the dock in San Francisco with my entire company. We all wore helmets, parade rest, and were loaded down with winter and summer gear. We were ready to embark. My name was called. I remember saying excuse me to the men in rank as I tried to get by with my equipment. Then I sat on my duffel and watched the others file aboard, bumping up the side of the ship, the cables flexing. I could see rust in the water being pumped from the bilge. Sailors laughed way over my head. It only took a few hours to load the troop. There were some people there to wave good-bye, though not for the soldiers since our shipping out was something secret.

Nothing was ever said. I was transferred to another unit where all the troops were baseball players. I played second base on the Third Army team. I batted seventh and bunted a lot. We traveled by train from one base to another in Texas, Georgia, and on up into New Jersey for the summer. We had a few cars to ourselves, including a parlor with an open platform. The rest of the train was made up of reefers full of frozen meat. The train was aluminum and streamlined. We could stand in the vestibules or in the open doorway of the baggage car where we kept the bags of bats and balls and the pinstriped uniforms hung on rods and look out over the pink flat deserts. There wouldn't be a cinder from the engine, its wheels a blur. You would see it up ahead on the slow curves, the white smoke of the whistle trailing back over the silver boxcars of meat and then the whistle. Some cars still had to be iced so we'd stop in sad, little towns, play catch and pepper while the blocks melted in the sun and the sawdust turned dark and clotty on the platform. We'd hit long fly balls to the local kids who'd hang around. We left them broken bats to nail and tape.

The meat was our duty. It was what we said we did even though everyone knew we played baseball. The Army wanted us to use frozen meat instead of fresh. We ran the tests in messes to see if the men could tell the difference. We stood by the garbage cans and took the plates to scrape and separate the scraps of meat to weigh for waste. A red plate meant the meat was fresh. The bone, the chewed gristle, the fat. I picked it out of the cold peas and potatoes. Sometimes whole pieces would come back, gray and hard. The gravy had to be wiped off before it went on the scale. Those halls were huge, with thousands of men hunched over the long tables eating. We stood by watching, waiting to do our job. It made no difference, fresh or frozen, to the man. This pleased the Army. Things were changing. Surplus from the war was being given to the U.N. for the action in Korea. There were new kinds of boots and rifles. Then every camp still had walk-in lockers. The sides of meat hung on racks. The cold blew through you. Blue inspection stamps bled into the yellow fat of the carcasses. All gone now. That's what I did in the service.

But the baseball didn't change. The ball still found my glove. There were the old rituals at home. I rubbed my hands in the dirt then wiped them on my pants, took the bat and rapped it on the plate. The pitch that followed always took me by surprise — hard and high, breaking away. The pitcher spun the ball like a dial on a safe. And trains still sound the same when they run through this town. At night, one will shake our house (we live near an overpass) and I can't go back to sleep. I'll count the men who walked up that gangway to the ship. The train's wheels squeal and sing. It might as well be hauling the cargo of my dreams.

What I See

I was killing time at the ranger station in West Glacier, twirling the postcard racks by the door. There was an old one of some teenagers around a campfire near Swift Current Lake. They have on dude ranch clothes, indigo jeans with the legs rolled into wide cuffs. The boys have flattops. There is a uke. One girl, staring into the fire, wears saddle shoes. The colors are old colors. Colors from the time women all wore red lipstick. Beyond the steel blue lake the white glaciers are smearing down the mountainsides. I saw the glaciers even though it was night in the card. They gave off their own light. No one ever took this card, not even as a joke. I was looking at this card when a woman walked in with her son. They mounted the stair above the model of the park. The models of the mountains were like piles of green and brown laundry, the glaciers sheets. The lakes were blue plastic. A red ribbon stood for the Going to the Sun Highway. It all looked manageable. The mother pointed. In the corner was the little house. You are here. She said to me then: Is there any place we can go to overlook the grizzlies?

This year the wolves have moved back into the park. And number 23 had mauled a camper, his third this year, but didn't kill her. Children walk through the station with bells on their feet. When the wind is right you can hear the songs drifting in from the higher trails. We were told there would be more people here this season because of the way the world has turned. There are too many people here for this place ever to be wild wild.

The cable's come as far as Cutbank. On my days off, I rent a room in town and watch the old movies they've juiced up with color. But the colors are as pale as an old rug. They look like they've already faded from old age. Now the blue sky outside looks manufactured, transported here from the other side of the mountain, its own conveyor belt. A bolt of dyed cloth. It is dripping with color. And my shorts here are khaki, which is Urdu for the word *dirt.* Sometimes my eyes hurt from seeing the situation so clearly. Every ten minutes or so I hear the ice tumble in the machine out on the breeze-way. Then the condenser kicks on. Out the window I can see back to the park, beyond the hot tableland to the mountains and the five white fingers of the glacier.

All of what I know about the world worms its way to me from Atlanta. The news is to stay put. They have a park in Atlanta. In it is the Cyclorama, a huge picture with no edges. The Battle of Atlanta is everywhere. The painting keeps wrapping around me so even out of the corners of my eyes I see nothing but the smoke and the smoky bodies falling about me. Atlanta is a mustard yellow in the distance. Sherman rides up in front of me. The battle ends and it begins again. I climb out of the painting through a hole in the floor. There is no place to overlook it. In the basement of the building is the famous steam locomotive The General. I see Ted Turner has just painted that movie.

And it strikes me now that I once looked like Buster Keaton, my campaign hat was tilted like his hat, as I stood next to King on the memorial steps. The monument behind us was white, even its shadows were white. King's suit had a sheen like feathers or skin. The white shirts glowed. Everyone wore white shirts except for my khaki since color hadn't been invented yet. The Muslims wore white. Their caps were white. And the crowd spilling down the steps looked like marble in white to stay cool. It was swampy near the river. They showed the speech around his birthday. I am always there, a ghost over his left shoulder. I was so young. I look as if nothing could surprise me. A ranger look. It always surprises me now. Now I know how it all came out, what happened to that man. I look like a statue. King flickers. I kept him in the corner of my eye. I watched the crowd. What I see is me seeing. I don't see what is coming. When they color it they will get the color of my eyes wrong.

In the window of the motel, I watch the day move. I have made a career with Interior. The range is being painted over by a deep blue sky. The glacier grips the mountaintop then lets go to form a cloud. Then everything just goes.

The Teakwood Deck
of the USS *Indiana*

I stabbed a man in Zulu. It had to do with a woman. I remember it was a pearled penknife I'd got from a garage. I'd used it for whittling and the letters were wearing off. It broke off in his thigh and nicked the bone. It must have hurt like hell.

I did the time in Michigan City in the metal shop, where I would brush on flux and other men would solder. Smoke would be going up all over the room. They made the denim clothes right there in the prison. The pants were as sharp as the sheet metal we were folding into dustpans and flour scoops. It was like I was a paper doll and they'd folded the jacket on me with the tabs creased over my shoulders. And the stuff never seemed to soften up but come back from the laundry shrunk and rumpled, just as stiff until the one time when all the starch would be gone and your clothes were rags and you got some new ones.

There was a man in there who was building a ship. When I first saw it, he had just laid down the keel and the hull looked like a shiny new coffin. This guy was in for life and he kept busy building a model of a battleship, the USS *Indiana.* He had hammered rejected license plates, flattened the numbers out. He'd fold and hammer. In the corner of the shop he'd pinned up the plans, a blue ship floated on the white paper. He had models made from balsa, the ribs showing through in parts. He had these molds of parts he would use to cast, jigs and dies. His tools were blades and snips. The needles he used to sew the tiny flags, he used in the model as antennae. The ship was 1/48th size of the real thing, as big as a canoe. The men who walked the deck had heads the size of peas. He painted each face differently, the ratings on their blue sleeves. He told me stories about each man frozen there on the bridge, here tucking into a turret, here popping out of a hatchway. He showed me letters from the same men. He had written to them sending samples of the paint he had mixed asking the men who had actually scraped and painted the real ship if this was anywhere near. He knew the hour, the minute, of the day his ship was sailing, the moment he was modeling.

But this was years later. At first I saw the hull. I saw the pile of rivets he collected from the temples of old eyeglasses. He collected spools for depth charges, straws for gun barrels, window screen for the radar. He collected scraps from the floor of the shop and stockpiled them near the ship. Toothpicks, thimbles, bars of soap, gum wrappers. Life Savers that were lifesavers, caps from tubes for valves and knobs, pins for shell casings. Everything was something else.

At first he started building only the ship but knew soon

enough he'd finish. So he went back and made each part more detailed, the guns and funnels, then stopped again and made even the parts of parts. The pistons in the engines, lightbulbs in the sockets.

Some men do this kind of thing. I whittled but I took a stick down to nothing. I watched the black knots of the branches under the bark grow smaller with each smooth strip until they finally disappeared. Maybe I'd sharpen the stick, but that got old. Finally it is the shavings thin like the evening paper at my feet. That was what I was after. Strip things so fine that suddenly there is nothing there but the edge of the knife and the first layer of skin over my knuckle.

One of the anchors of the real battleship is on the lawn of the Memorial Coliseum in Fort Wayne. The anchor is gray and as big as a house. I took my then wife to see it. We looked around that state for the other one. But only found deck guns on lawns of the VFW, a whole battery at the football stadium near the university. In other towns, scrap had been melted and turned into statues of sailors looking up and tiny ships plowing through lead waves.

The deck of the model was the only real thing. He said the wood was salvaged from the deck. A guard brought him a plank of it. He let me plane it, strip the varnish and splinter it into boards. A smell still rose from it of pitch, maybe the sea. And I didn't want to stop. I've seen other pieces of the deck since then in junior high schools made into plaques for good citizens. It is beautiful wood. The metal plates engraved with names and dates are bolted on, and near the bottom there is another smaller one that says this wood is from the deck of the battleship. It is like a piece of the true cross. And that is why I came to the capitol in Indianapolis to see the governor's desk. I heard it was made from the teakwood deck of the USS *Indiana.*

So imagine my surprise when in the rotunda of the building I find the finished model of the ship in a glass case with a little legend about the prisoner in Michigan City. He'd finished it before he'd died. The porthole windows were cellophane cut from cigarette packs. The signal flags spelled out his name. It was painted that spooky gray, the color between the sea and sky, and in the stern a blue airplane was actually taking off and had already climbed above the gleaming deck where a few seamen waved.

I felt sad for that con. He spent his life building this. He never got it right. It wasn't big enough or something.

I walked right into the governor's office. I'm a taxpayer. And the lady told me he wasn't there, but I told her I was more interested in the desk. So she let me in. "It's beautiful, isn't it?" she said, opening the curtains for the light that skidded across the top cut to the shape of the state. One edge was pretty straight and the other, where the river ran, looked as if that end had melted like a piece of butter into toast. I was running my hand along the length of it, feeling how smooth it was — the grain runs north and south — when the governor walked in with his state trooper.

"It's something," he said. He's a Republican. The trooper followed and stood behind him. "It has its own light."

The trooper wore a sea blue uniform with sky blue patches at the shoulders and the cuffs. Belts hung all over him. Stripes and creases ran down his legs. Braids and chains. The pants were wool. He watched me. And I looked at him.

Jesus, you've got to love a man in uniform.

I stepped up to the desk and saw my face and the shadow of my body deep inside the swirling wood. I took my finger and pointed to the spot not far from Zulu where I knifed a man and said, "Right there." I pushed hard with my nail. "That's where I was born."

Limited

I saw the rock, saw the boy who threw it. I saw it hit the window next to the seat in front of me. Saw the window shatter instantly. Saw that now I couldn't see through the window anymore. And we were gone out of Warsaw on the Broadway Limited. We hadn't stopped at Warsaw but gone through at sixty miles an hour. I saw the boy and the rock and his friends around him on their bicycles, and I imagined our train rocking the town, pushing the sound of the horn ahead along the tracks. Not stopping.

Now the whole car, everyone, is talking and pointing at the window. There is a high-pitched whistle. The light is different in the window since the windows are tinted. And the guy who sits there has just come back from the club car, dumb with luck, not drunk enough yet. I could have been sitting there, he says again. Everyone is talking about the kid with the rock and the window and outside now are cornfields and a few houses and the highway far away.

The conductor is looking out the rear door of this last car, and it looks like he is shaving. He is not shaving but whispering into a radio while he looks back at the tracks coming together. I saw the rock, saw the boy, I tell him. He says that it's not the first time. Called someone who'll call the police. He's an old man. He's seen it all. He can't understand it.

I saw the rock float along with us at our speed, saw it barely catch up to us. I saw the boys on the bikes holding up their arms, jubilant, already tearing away from the place. The window went white.

He waited. Waited for the engines and the baggage cars, the coaches, the dome, the sleepers, the diner, the cafe. He waited, the rock already in his hand. More sleepers, more coaches, this last car. He waits, sees the people in the windows. Something so big and so much metal. Silver and blue. His whole town shaking. One long horn. He can't hear his friends egging him on. This rock won't stop a thing, won't slow nothing down. He throws it, and it's gone.

Three Tales of the Sister City

I

If the Chamber of Commerce had known the chef was arriving on the last United flight that evening someone would surely have been there to welcome him.

At first he waited near the doors that led out to the apron and the parked airplanes. It was raining. The airport is not equipped with the ramps that connect the planes to the terminal. Instead, passengers that night were given red, white, or blue umbrellas.

He looked outside. In the dark, he could see only the huge umbrellas bobbing, the colored panels and the white ones stained red by the flashing lights of the electric carts unloading the luggage. The umbrellas floated back to the airplane and up the metal stairs. The rain was a sheet on the white fuselage.

Passengers entered the terminal. A man in coveralls collected the umbrellas. Some were left open and some closed but not rolled. He hugged the umbrellas to his chest. Water dripped down the leg of his pantsuit. After a bit, the man ran back out through the rain, rocking the bundle of umbrellas, three of them still open and shooting out about him. He pushed up the stairs to deliver the umbrellas to a steward handing them to passengers at the door of the airplane. In the terminal some angry men shoved the umbrellas from themselves as they came in the door. The umbrellas flew across the waiting room, hitting chairs and skidding over the floor. They kicked at the umbrellas on the floor. The carpet was dark from the water.

The chef stood near the door, waiting for someone to come up to him, umbrellas scattered around him. He was dressed in a white uniform — shoes, pants, tunic. The kerchief he wore when he worked at a table was in his pocket. He wore a white hat. His hair was wet. The only English he knew was *Don Hall,* the man who opened Takaoka, the restaurant named for our sister city, and who had invited him here. There were small groups of loud people all around him in the corridor. He went on up the ramp to claim his luggage.

The new conveyor wound around the room. The belt skimmed along just above the floor, curved back on itself, bulged, detoured around ceiling columns. The suitcases and flight bags went from one clutch of people to another, sniffed at their heels for an owner, wheeled around, meandered toward a businessman with a coat over his shoulder, and then disappeared behind the rubber strips in the wall.

His bags did not appear.

He stared at the black sheets moving by his feet. Only the

women at the rental desk remained — red, green, orange, yellow — placing envelopes in lighted boards on the walls. There were a few men at telephones.

At last, the small case that held his knives appeared at his feet. The bright yellow tag had been placed on its handle. The knives had been taken away as he boarded a plane. He had tried to explain. They had given him a yellow tag instead.

He chased after the case, catching up to it in a few strides. Together they waited for more luggage. The conveyor stopped. Across the empty room he saw a few clumps of unclaimed luggage, none of it his.

Later that evening, he was in a restaurant kitchen. It wasn't clear that this was the restaurant where he was to work. He had been saying Don Hall to everyone, and now he was in a restaurant and here he felt more at home. The woman who had shown him to the kitchen sat across from him at the shining steel table. The kitchen had been cleaned at closing, and the metal sang in the bright light. There were chrome panels on the walls, woven aluminum racks, nickel trim on the oven doors. The sinks, the freezer doors, the shelves stacked with bone china were of stainless. He was stirring the burnishing balls with his hand. He lifted a dozen to his face, let them spill through his fingers back into the bright tin can. The drains were minted coins set into the floor.

The woman had been gesturing all the time. She lifted a silver hood on one of the tables. He saw tubs of butters and white pastes, yellow and red sauces, shaved meats and dried cheeses. She placed before him a loaf of bread and a pale green head of lettuce.

He opened his case and took out his knives, crossing two before him on his oiled cutting board. He held the head of lettuce in both hands for a second then set it down firmly as if he were setting a stone.

He cut into the little finger of his left hand on one of the first slices through the lettuce but did not realize it. There were drops of blood on the almost white leaves. He saw the darker veins running through the pale leaf.

The woman ran for help. He pressed the wound against the leg of his pants. He still wasn't afraid, but he was alone again.

2

The man who was the official photographer for the Chamber came from one of those countries that has no language of its own.

He was the last known immigrant to the city.

He was taking pictures of the summer parade and was allowed to walk in the street. The children on the curb were waving Japanese flags. He wore several cameras, each with different lenses.

In the parade, the ambassadors from our sister city rode in a yellow bus. They wore blue kimonos and leaned out through the open windows. They took pictures of the children on the curb waving the Japanese flags. Their wide blue sleeves swung along the yellow sides of the bus. Red lights flashed.

He saw her in the window beneath the black image of a bird. A black pinstripe ran the length of the bus. He walked along taking her picture — her white face, her black hair, the blue kimono and the knot of the white obi.

When she arrived at his house that evening, he could barely hide his disappointment. She wore Western dress. In the basement where he had his studio and darkroom he showed her the framed pictures of his daughter that hung on every wall.

She turned from one picture, touched her own breast, and pointed at his daughter. He looked down through his glasses, his head tilted away, at his daughter's chest. He saw, for the first time, a second set of small dark nipples beneath her full breasts. They had been there all the time.

He turned back to the woman, who now looked at the popcorn she held in her cupped hands. She brought the popcorn up to her face and with her tongue took one kernel into her mouth. Some other kernels had fallen on the wood table below her knees, and he saw that each kernel looked like an orchid. Their metallic throats were the fragments of the shell, the seed turned inside out.

3

We had no way of knowing they were mad at each other. When they arrived in Fort Wayne, we thought they looked enough alike to be brothers.

At our noon meetings at the Chamber, they uncrated the boxes that had been delivered that day. They held up shovels and brushed off the packing straw; they oiled the clippers while we watched. We saw the rakes and the brooms, the trowels and the hods. When the boulders began to arrive they took turns telling stories of discovering each stone, of wanting that one to go to America, to the Sister City. The stones spoke saying so.

Everything followed. The smaller rocks and the pebbles in jars, the envelopes of pine needles, the stone lanterns, the bamboo pipe. The plants and the trees were waved through customs. Even some water came from Japan with a note from the mayor.

They were given a backhoe to use and instructions on how to run it. They were shown the stretch of yard east of the Performing Arts Building that had been set aside.

And they worked well enough together, setting stones, the dwarf pines, the creeping evergreens. It began to take shape in our minds.

Then they started fighting. They knocked over piles of rock, stepped on the dam of pebbles and sand they had made to form the pools. They stopped people as they walked from the parking lots to work.

"This or this?" they asked. "This or this?" No one knew what to do. They worked on opposite sides of the plot, and we heard that they threatened each other with tools. We watched from office buildings. People took sack lunches outside and watched for the hour. Sides were being taken. Pools and lotteries were being formed. Bets placed. We talked of little else.

No one could talk to them. They stopped talking to each other. Our local architect, the men from the city greenhouse, the women who had taken the flower arranging course in our sister city all tried to explain to them how we felt.

Really, we could see no difference between them. It all looked Japanese. We liked the colors next to the red brick of the building.

Finally one of them abandoned the project site altogether, drove the backhoe to another part of the newly sodded lawn, and started digging. The other one paid no attention, poured goldfish into the shallow pond.

The delegation had come from Takaoka to escort the gardeners home. At the airport the Japanese were dressed to the hilt. We all bowed to say good-bye. We muttered a few words we knew. We had arranged ourselves around the brown waiting area and kept the two of them far apart. They sat silently, heads bowed. All of us pretended none of this had happened.

The runway stretched on and on.

A woman from our city broke the silence, suggested that we sing the state song, that everyone should sing. The out-of-town businessmen stood up, charmed by the silk and smiles.

We pretended to sing. The woman had a clear, high voice. She sang the state song — a song about the rivers, the trees, the meadows, the hills, the unimproved beauty of our state.

Guam

The time in Indiana never changes. I grew up minutes from the Ohio line, and in the spring, the clocks leapt forward there. But in Indiana we'd lose an hour without trying.

A pack of us in my father's Olds crossed over to Van Wert and a bar there called Mr. Entertainer and got smashed on 3.2 beer, legal for minors. In the summers the nights were long, longer than the bars were open, and we waited for the dawn, parked on some township road, the car wading in the corn. It was the funniest thing to us, buzzed as we were, to race the sun back to Indiana. There were five guys in the backseat. We took off, the tail of my father's car dragging in the gravel. Even floored, it took a quarter section before the overdrive cut in, and then, maybe, we hit a grade at an intersection or the road tossed us up when it switched to tar or oil. The shocks heaved, and we were flying, the eight knocking and the tires revving off the ground. This was dawn. Maybe there was a farmer on a Case, scything the ditch weed with a sickle bar. All of us stuck our arms out the windows, flapping our wings. I blew the horn, and we watched ourselves pass the sound. We saw it roll off the fenders and tumble into the dust, bounce a few times behind us like something we'd killed. We were moving so fast, we weren't moving, like the times all of us had sat in our fathers' parked cars and pretended to drive, that fast. And then we jumped over another road and into Indiana, and there, it was an hour before we left the bar, and we felt like we had cheated on several things and gotten away with it all.

I could tell this hadn't impressed her. A frat house friend from college had set us up. This was the year after graduation, when I was sharing an apartment the company owned with some other guys. It was on the west side of New York City, and for the first couple of weeks I lived there I watched the sun set in a smudge on the other side of the river at the end of our street. Her name was Doreen, and this was the only time I ever took her out.

"So, where you from, Doreen?" I asked. We were walking around Times Square looking for something to do.

"We moved around a lot," she said.

This was kind of a lie, I found out. Later, at the comedy club where we ended up, all the comics taking turns at the open mic started their routines by telling us we were a good-looking crowd and asking us where we were from.

"Guam!" Doreen shouted louder than the rest of us could shout where we were from. And all the comics picked her out of the noise of states and cities.

"You're kidding. You're from Guam!" they'd say, adjusting the microphone stand to their height. Guam is a funny enough word, and they all had jokes they'd fire off as they settled into their timing and material.

Doreen rolled her drink between her hands. Her neck snapped back when she laughed. Things dangled from her ears. She'd say, "Guam!" when the next guy came on and asked, nervous and squinting in the lights, where we were from. And Guam again for the guy after that. It was funny because none of the comics had heard the one before him, passing the time in the greenroom backstage. So the last several were getting laughs just for throwing off the question. The house sat still to let Doreen answer the question he had forgotten, in the silence, he had asked. "Guam! I'm from Guam!" and the comic would recover with a joke about food or sex, thanking her with his eyes and the cock of his head for such a straight line. But by this time I couldn't laugh anymore because I had laughed so much already at all the other comics who'd come before. They had been funny. I felt bad that the only way to let the last ones know they were funny was to laugh, and I just couldn't anymore.

It was early in the morning when we left. A new comic was asking what remained of the audience where they were from. We started walking home.

"So, what was Guam like?" I asked Doreen. I imagined island beaches of ground volcanoes, cinder-block houses painted after-dinner mint colors, reefs made from rusted hulks of sunken ships. Everyone is related and looks the same.

"I was only born there," Doreen said. "I'm from no place really. But I remember it like every place else I've lived. Quonset huts, lots of Quonset huts."

It was early in the morning, and I was trying to think how to get us to an after-hours club downtown my roommate had told me about. There, no one would expect me to laugh, just dance and drink, and I could get close to Doreen and shout in her ear, ask her more questions she wouldn't answer. I still didn't know then how the night would turn out.

Tomorrow's market in Tokyo had already closed. Hong Kong had fixed the price of gold. Their yesterdays already heading this way. In my office, I kept a laundered shirt in my desk drawer. No need to go home. There were no cabs. There never are. We were standing on a traffic island in the middle of Broadway, back to back and circling each other, concentrating on the cars as they rushed by. Above us, the lights of the big signs sputtered all around. I began my story about where I was from and what I did when I was there. I thought about Guam again while I was talking. I thought of the surge of water the moon pushes ahead of itself every day, bearing down on that pile of sand. And I thought about the people there, just getting up or just going to bed, laughing at each other, never thinking that I was thinking about them, here and at this very moment on the other side of the world.

The War That Never Ends

That summer I followed the trucks as they cut down the trees. I sold ice cream to the kids who watched, drawn by the pitch of the chain saws and the wood chipper. Our convoy snaked through the terraced neighborhoods. The green city two-and-a-half, the cherry picker folded on top, hauled the chipper, a yellow cannon. And trailing behind, the dump truck, its bed mounded with chips, pulled the leggy circular saw skirted with canvas that ground down the stumps. The trucks' lights flashed. They bucked in low gear. Their drivers rode the brakes, looking for the trees marked with the white X's. I pedaled hard behind them, thumbing the bells when I thought about it, jacking the freezer box back and forth as I cranked up a hill. I breathed in their trail of sickly sweet fresh-cut green wood and burned sap. The trees arched over us, leafless and dying.

More kids banged out of the screen doors, clutching change in their fists. They jumped on their chipped bikes and swerved in behind me. Their axle cleaners, strips of leather riveted together with a cheap reflector, plunked the spokes of their wheels when we coasted, sounding like a flat Oriental instrument.

I sold chocolate bombs with soft centers and Popsicle rockets I broke in two on the edge of the cart, plugs of ribboned ice cream in paper cups they ate with flat wooden spoons that came wrapped in wax paper I ripped from a belt, tubes of orange Push-Ups with pointed sticks, fudge bars that crusted over white in the humidity, sandwiches with the wafers peeling in strips, and Dreamsicles evaporating into thin air. The kids sat on the curbs, a splatter of drips around their feet in the gutters. A man in a bucket up in the trees tied a cable around the biggest limb while men on the ground snipped off branches with the long-handled pruners. The foreman, wearing a tie, pointed to the place he wanted the trunk to fall. I let a piece of dry ice smoke on the lid of the box.

I needed the money to stay in college and out of the draft. The Popsicles sold for 7 cents. I cleared a penny after the rent on the trike. I had thought about enrolling in a safe academy, the Coast Guard or the Merchant Marine, waiting out the war learning to shoot stars and spend my summers on long training cruises aboard old minesweepers made of wood and nonmagnetic metals. I had too many fillings to get in, cavities being a general indication of health, the applications said. Then, they could afford to be choosy.

"You sure you want that?" I said. The little boys still had their milk teeth. They stood around the cart and sucked the red syrup from the cherry pop, turning it into a chunk of pink ice on a stick. An older girl ran back home with the grimy change and a Drumstick for her mother, who stood in the shade of her front door.

The trees came apart so easily. Two or three chain saws whined at once. Then one idled, putting, as its operator considered his next cut. The sawdust sifted down. Leg-length logs were lowered by rope like scenery on a stage. In the street a man swept the dust and twigs into neat piles with a new push broom, tapping the stiff bristles twice after each swipe.

The chipper ran on its own engine, chewing up the logs and brittle branches. The man on the ground hurled the wood into the blades like he was throwing spears. They caught and the engine coughed and almost stalled until the grinding drum inside bit in and screamed, ripping through the limbs that shot out in shreds up the stack. It had a rhythm like the locusts in the trees at night, and the sound brought the mothers out to watch. I sat waiting, flicking the tinkly bells on the handlebar between the wails that sounded above the sputtering engine. A mother drifted up to my cart and bought something and watched until the trunk crashed down and was sectioned into wheels and rolled away. All the time she held the mushy wrapper away from her body. Then she threw the stained stick on the piles of sawdust and brown leaves.

The houses had been shaded, softened by the canopy above. Now after the trees were cut the houses looked stark and new again, just built, the lawn bald where the children had played. The sky lifted, and I could make out the shapes of dormers and eaves and see the sickly TV antennas twisted on the roofs, saplings that didn't survive the winter.

I had lived through an age of service. Bread trucks delivered then. Men sharpened knives at your door. There were brushes for everything. Milk in bottles appeared on the stoop. The milk cartons now are printed with faces of newsboys who've disappeared. They identify the dead with dental records. All that summer the trees kept dying, and the city crews, their saws calling back and forth to each other, cut every elm.

I didn't cheat the war but went. In the cities they blew up trucks with hand grenades dropped into fuel tanks. A rubber band held the plunger in until the gas dissolved the rubber. There were always two explosions in Saigon. The first to bring the crowd. The streets were filled with bicycles. As they flowed by me, they made a soft sawing sound as soft as chirping crickets.

When I came home, I rode a bike along streets I didn't recognize. The trees the city planted, the ginkgos and the crimson maples, had filled in. Along the fences the Chinese elms sprayed up, weeds, from all the trimming. The houses were smaller. The hills were steeper. The telephone poles still towered above the new trees, their cables sagging. At one pole a wire angled out from the top and ran to the ground. A long time ago the wire had grown into a tree branch. When they cut that tree down, they cut on either side of the wire, leaving the gray slice behind, still suspended, floating above me. Straddling my bike, I stood there awhile keeping that disk of wood between me and the sun, trying to imagine the time it took for the tree to absorb the wire. The wire hasn't let go, even now when the disease is dead.

Chatty Cathy Falls
into the Wrong Hands

Let me tell you that the boys who stole me from Baby Face, lusting after the secret of this voice, their own hearts racing when they screwed their eyes down to the scale of my dress tipping the scales that shut mine, as good as they were with their hands, came away disappointed when all they found after they found no easy way in (and they had ways) was a whorl of perforations in my chest more like a pattern left by a mustard plaster or a Band-Aid than the actual ventilation of my views; and I told them all I was admitting was sound, all I was allowing was conversation as they tossed me away without so much as another word like a live grenade seconds before I blew, pin pulled out, as if I had the short fuse, armed and fertile as I was without a loop to hang on; if they only would have stopped to hear what I had to say instead of hearing their own inarticulate insides, I would have told them how things work in this world, all right; can a man imitate speech? I ask you; I was born talking, talking borne, wired and whining, content enough to be a thing itself, a person and a place, made to lie on my back and run on, coming to understand why those boys were so uncomfortable with the hollow part of language, and imagining a woman who talks too much; and I find that even if, after plugging me a time or two, the boys had decided to unscrew my noggin to look inside, to uncoil what was left of this doll's notion and then send my Fuller Brush head back to Baby Face on a Mattel tea plate with my eyes rolled up inside my brain, a replica of screams, a fabrication (after all) of speech playing dumb, I would, always, even as we speak, let that other part of me go on talking (listen to me) until the line runs in.

Evaporation

Your mother can't even remember why I never drink. She sits upstairs by the bedroom window until the timed diamond lights switch off, repeats every question I ask her.

"What are you doing?"

"What are you doing?" she says.

Kids on bikes racing on the infield drag clouds of dirt from base to base. The softball players drink beer in the stands, telling each other stories about the game they have just played. Their voices carry. It's against park rules. It's a public park.

"They shouldn't be drinking."

"They shouldn't be drinking," your mother says, her face reflected like smoke in the window. I had turned on the light on the chest of drawers to write some letters while I was thinking of it. One to Bill Kaple down at the City Light and another to the reporter I like at WKJG. The next morning, I went and picked up the beer cans from beneath the bleachers, filled the yellow fifty-gallon drum the park board leaves for trash. I flicked out the dregs from each can onto the dust.

The beer dribbled into shimmering balls of gray powdered mud almost like mercury before the ground got dry again.

I've told you how in 1930 I was working for the Pennsy when the foreman said, "We're going to have to lay you off, Jimmy." I was a management trainee, but that day I was a gandy dancer learning the ropes. "Just for a little while," he said. I wasn't called back until 1938, but by that time I was working for the City Light, turning off the electricity when people ran up their light bills while they were paying down their gas bills and setting meters again when they paid off the light bill. But I was lucky in 1930, when they laid me off from the Pennsy. I got another job right away as an orderly at the Irene Byron outside of town. I had to live on the grounds, in the ward and come home only on the weekend. I left you and your mother early every Sunday and walked up the Kendallville Road, out into the country to the county farm and the children's home to the sanatorium where I wheeled the TB patients through the big French doors out onto the screened-in porches even in winter.

I listened to them breathe on those cold nights, the moon throwing shadows of the screens like a net over their wrapped up bodies. Their breath smoked. The screens rattled in their frames when the wind blew. The big engines of the night trains on the Big Four track slipped climbing the steep grade behind the powerhouse, lost their head of steam and panted up the hill.

This was before the repeal of Prohibition. Hospitals were granted an allowance for evaporation of the alcohol they could use. We all knew this. Most of the orderlies stole a teaspoon or two from each big jug, the theft disguised as a part of the fraction that was lost naturally. I kept a Nehi bottle hidden in the steam tunnels too. The tunnels connected all the wards and the cottages to the powerhouse. We used them in winter to go from place to place. The pipes hissed at the joints and sweated hugging the wet walls underground. A few bulbs strung overhead lit the junctions where the tunnels forked off with little puddles of light. I saw the sparkle of other bottles stuffed behind a knot of valves or beneath the wooden duckboard on the floor. I wrapped my bottle in asbestos batting so it looked like a section of discarded scrap pipe.

Your mother doesn't remember this. We lived then with your grandmother, who was failing, and once you all had to hide behind the curtains when the landlord came for the rent. I collapsed those weekends after the long walk home from the country. Your mother forgets, forgets how we worried, how we saved everything, and how I told her the alcohol accumulated drop by drop, more than a swallow, past a couple of fingers.

Those nights I slept with her I listened to her breathe. I woke up after midnight, screwed up from the shift I worked. Her breathing catches when she sleeps, not so much a snore as a click back in her throat that sounds like a clock ticking or a leaky faucet. And I figured in every exchange of air we were losing something. We were falling behind. Soon the act of breathing itself wouldn't be worth a good goddamn. I was so tired. Some nights finally I hoped she wouldn't be able to persuade herself to try again just settle into a last long sigh. I held my breath those nights so I could hear her, hear if this was it or this one or the next. But then the room would lighten enough for me to see the blankets rise and fall, and I had to leave before you even woke up to make it back to the sanatorium in time.

I told you how we went to a party after the repeal, how things were looking up. The alcohol we skimmed was still illegal but in a different way now. The party was out in Huntington. We were going to drink it all, toast the end of our bootlegging. Ed Patton, who's passed away now, and I took the first belt. We were lucky. We had eaten a lot of potato salad, ham sandwiches, and deviled eggs while we mixed together the hooch in a washtub, cutting it with lime rickey. Somebody had replaced the grain alcohol we stole with the rubbing kind, and both of us were out cold before we knew it. I've told you this. I came to under the kitchen sink. Back then there were three pipes — one for the hot, one for the cold, and one for something I can't remember. I woke looking up at those bars and knew I was in jail.

"Ed," I had said to him after taking the first swallow, "this is sure hard to get down." It's the last thing I remember before the pipes. They pumped my stomach and Ed's too. He froze both his feet later at the Battle of the Bulge and in the hospital then all the doctors asked him if he was related to the general, and he just said, "Hell, no!"

That was my last party and an end to all my drinking. People had come drunk to it, drunk on moonshine rye and smuggled Canadian whiskey. Perry Monet said he could walk a straight line and walked straight over the kitchen table and up and over the back of the davenport and on out the door and into the backyard. Your mother and Marcella Voltz put Forest Norton in the ringer washer and turned it on. He went around and round. I never knew who switched the alcohol. He might have been at the party, already pissed from the real stuff, too scared or stupid to say a word. I've been a sober man ever since.

At the sanatorium, one thing I had to do was massage the patients. I remember the chill it left on my hands when I swabbed the rubbing alcohol over someone's back, the way the skin drew up tight. From then on the vapor always made me a little sick, so I held my breath until I could feel the skin turn rough and warm. A doctor explained it to me once, how a liquid warms to the degree it takes to turn it to air and how it stays at the temperature, even if you add more heat, until the liquid's all gone.

Not much later, I was walking the alleys for the City Light. Tramps had scrawled these picture messages in chalk on the utility poles. *A dishonest man lives here.* A circle with an X inside marked a house good for a handout. A jagged line of triangles meant to tell a pitiful story. A bunch of lines was food for chores. You learned to draw the smiling cat you found scribbled on the paving bricks behind our house on Oakland Street. A kindhearted woman, a kindhearted woman lives here. You listened to the men on the back steps while they ate their fried egg sandwiches your mother made for them. And those weekend nights when I was home, you told me their stories, and they were always the same, how they'd heard of work in town, how they had a kid like you at home.

People waited. Once I had to shut off the power to a house on Brandroff Street. The meter was in the basement. I had to go through a bulkhead in the back. In the backyard around a card table were six or seven men all out of work playing euchre or watching the game. They stopped and turned toward me, looked at me standing in a clump of hollyhocks and ashes while the tenant fiddled with the lock on the door. I expected something would happen, for them to run me off. Instead they spent the moment just staring at me, as if I wasn't worth the effort. The patients too, on the breezeways and porches, shrinking inside their rugs, watched the moon rise and then set. And your mother, back then, sitting with her mother, trying to pry her mouth open with a spoonful of broth.

Your mother sleeps all the time now, even in the chair beside the window. In the park, a yellow tractor comes each day to drag the field smooth again with an old piece of chain-link fence. The cloud of dust it raises drifts this way. I try to remember when it started happening, how we got to here. That ratchet in her throat cranks her head down, her chin to her chest.

"Blanche," I say, "Blanche, wake up."

She starts. "Wake up," she says. "Wake up."

And I try to think of something more to say.

Miners

Going east, I cross the Ohio by a bridge that empties on the west side, smack into a mountain face tunneled through to Wheeling. Set back from the highway on the old roadbeds are the miners' houses. Mountains are at their back doors. The highway cuts through the mountains, and on the sheer faces of the cliffs on both sides, I see where they've bored and set the charges like a pencil split in two and the lead removed.

I think about the products of coal. The stockings you wear. The records you play. The aspirin you take. The pencil you write with. These are mine. What would we do without carbon?

The face of the land is changing. I am going east so I can write to you.

The hillsides are quarries mining men. The men are going home, where they will discover that all the waters in Shakespeare will not clean them. This life has gotten under their skins. They make love in smudges.

I am going further east, where men are inside of things, where they own things inside and out.

I am writing this with a pencil painted yellow and printed with a silhouette of a woman with no arms.

I wish I were a miner so that when you turned your back to me and the face of the land changed, before I would go back underground, I would reach out and write with my black finger some graphite text on the places you could not reach.

"You," it would say, "are mine."

The War of
Northern Aggression

Sometimes we are mistaken for Nazis. We are not Nazis. It is our blond hair. It is our white skins. The names are not Latin. Johnston, Buell, Early, and Jackson. We speak English to each other when we wish not to be understood. We marry our cousins and stay within the walls of our villas. We have been here generations now, but cannot forget the country we have left behind. Our ancestors burned their ships in the harbors. Pilgrims, my friend. But do not call us Yankees. Never call us Yankees.

We have traveled to Bogotá from our homes in the mountains to see the North American Vice Presidents when they make their state visits. We are curious about such men. We watch as the campesinos pelt the limousines with eggs and paving stones from the plazas. I myself liked Señor Nixon, his face the color of newsprint. How he smiled and waved even as the masses swamped his sweating blue Cadillac.

For a while we grew rubber. Then for a long time bananas, but the bananas are all dying now. You do not know this yet in the north. A fungus infests the plantations, staining the leaves of the trees. The plants are all of the same variety, interbred, like us, our white flesh like the flesh of the banana, vulnerable to such things. We collect the toy Spanish horses now, grow a little coffee and broker chocolate, even some cotton. We grow the cashew, too, along with other crops.

My family owned land outside of Atlanta. Sherman slept there, my granddaddy told the children, one night during the siege. Refusing the master bedroom, he pitched a tent in the gardens. Tara, yes, like the movie. The flowers bloomed and the sky turned red with flame. I have never been there. My picture of the mansion comes from the books of the time, little Greek temples surrounded by weeping trees. I think of the Acropolis in Athens, where I have been on business, the white porches and the fluted columns. When I was there, they were restoring the Parthenon, encased in scaffolding, not to the way it looked before the Turks blew it up but to its previous state of decay. It had grown shabby. It had melted like a cake in the heat of the exhaust, the *nephos* the Greeks call it, the cloud of smoke. I think of the house in Atlanta that way. Still smoldering, always smoldering. The white walls scorched and pocked from countless bullets. Zouaves, who look like Turks, are carrying away the portraits of my forebears and their dogs. The slaves, dazed, attach themselves as contraband to the Union invader.

Now, we sing the old hymns in English still. Here, where we feel in our bones, the seasons in reverse, we grow nostalgic. We have avoided our whole history by leaving the south of the north. We import cases of Coca-Cola from Atlanta for our cotillions in the fall, where I wear the moth-eaten gray and yellow tunic of my great-granddaddy. The ladies, caged in ancient contraptions of whalebone and browning silk, sip from the heavy glass bottles of Coke. The salted peanuts blanch, dissolve in the dregs of the flat black syrup.

We watch the burning of Atlanta every year on television. We know the lines of the movie by heart. The satellite dish is in the nearest grove of our dying banana trees. The rotting leaves collect in its shallow palm, breaking up reception. On our screens, the scratchy snow is an image of the mosaic disease infecting our dying banana trees. Today on CNN, through bursts of static, we watched the pictures of North American helicopters settling in our own jungles like falling leaves. The *guardia* set fire to the bales of coca. Then we looked out of our windows and saw the coiling trunks of the new forest of smoke, growing on the slopes of the blue hills beyond. And then you came to take us back with you.

Listen, no place is home but this home for us. You North Americans should know how we feel. To be extraditable. A nation such as yours made up of people who have come from elsewhere, you should know. But you forget, you forget, my friend, the bitter taste of leaving for good. For who has left the garden of North America once they have arrived? Here, we still celebrate the Fourth of July by not noticing its passing, still mourning the fall of Vicksburg long ago. We Southerners are one example. We left and never thought to go back. And there is the colony of free black men and women all named Doe, whom we think of as kin, killing each other as we speak in their postage stamp country on the green equatorial shores of western Africa.

Elkhart, There,
at the End of the World

The roads are lined with produce stands. There is no cider or ear corn as there would be in the early fall but the feral fruit of midsummer, strawberries and melons. Little is left in the shacks — empty wicker quarts and pecks, fragile chain scales, U-Pick-Em signs. I head toward Elkhart, Indiana, where reed and brass instruments are made. The wind whistles through the car, and I follow a station wagon of migrant workers, tailgate down, leaking the brown exhaust of legs and arms, up from the Lincoln Highway toward Michigan to cherries and tomatoes. I pass the sod farms where the sprinklers stutter and the overhead systems, struts and hoses, walk with water across the turf to the ruled black strips left after the grass is rolled away.

In Elkhart I stop for a train. Somewhere Conn makes clarinets and trumpets and the good high school bands have their pick of instruments. The marching bands spend their summers in travel and parades in all the nearby towns.

The train skates for Chicago as parts of houses back up

the street behind me. Tractors pulling trailers of modular homes, "Oversize Load" attached to their bumpers. The stalled lead cars and the trailing cars flash their yellow warning lights. We wait and the wind comes up to stir the red pennants and the clear plastic sheets that cover the open half of houses.

Somewhere in the middle of this I think that there is a place that produces a lasting thing. What stays when even the earth gets up and moves away? It is the season when the hot sky touches the ground and draws the water away. The earth cools too quickly and things keep moving toward high wind, tornadoes.

The train squeals by, and across the right-of-way the flat sound of siding dins again from the trailer factories. A bottom to the wind.

A horn. A horn. I move.

Blue Hair

Mister Pepe lowers the clear plastic canopy over my head, flicks a few switches, the engines throb to life. My blue hair, woven into whistling rollers, a snug helmet, bristles with bobby pins. The women on either side of me thumb through their magazines, but I am flying, flying over the checkerboard of friendly fields. The leafy woods below look like mats of hair on a linoleum floor. The engines roar. My wingmen tuck in beside me, our staggered flight piecing together the formation of the whole bomb group. Now the contrails peel off our leading edges. We bank together, coming to the heading that will take us back to the Ruhr. The sky, severely clear. Mister Pepe pokes a puffy cloud with his rat-tail comb. The starched white cliffs of Dover drape away below us. The flashing sliver of shears darts in and out. Nimble pursuit planes. Escorts with belly tanks nipping at our stragglers.

Years ago, I knew the war was over when the bombers left the plants with their aluminum skins unpainted. No need to camouflage the Boeings with that European forest green. It was only a matter of time. Hair, too, a matter of time. My hair would grow back. I watched as wave after wave of silver Forts lumbered over, climbed above the sound, the pounding of their engines rattling the bones in my head, my bare neck chilled by the breeze blowing in off the water.

"The hair, it is dead," Mister Pepe whispered in my ear. This was later when I first came here. He rinsed my hair of color, the tarnished yellow coiling down the drain. He had me peer into a microscope in the back room of his salon. Curling in behind me, he tweezed the knobs on the machine. I saw the shaft of the hair he had plucked from my scalp rip apart then reassemble, watched as my sight dove right through the splitting hair, my vision melting then turning hard.

"There," I said when it came into view, kinked and barked like a tree limb, blue as ice.

"Let me see," Mister Pepe said, wedging in to look. "It is damaged, no? The overtreated hair. The frazzled ends. You need my help, yes?"

And years before that the general had said, "You cannot tell anyone why you cut your hair." I was a young girl in Seattle. My parents stood in the doorway of our kitchen hugging each other as they watched the WAC snip a few locks. She held them up to the light, then draped the strands across the outstretched arms of a warrant officer. He slid the hair through his fingers, stretched it out straight, and lowered it into a box like the one florists use for long-stemmed roses.

I was a blond, and my hair had never been crimped or

permed or ironed. I never knotted it up into braids, only trimmed the fraying. It was naturally straight. I brushed it every night a hundred times and shampooed it with eggs and honey. When I slept, my hair nestled in behind me like another person slipping up against my back as I breathed, a heavy purring weight.

"It's a secret," the WAC had said, evening the ends. "Let me look at you." She held my chin in her palm, her fingers squeezing my cheeks. "You look all grown up now. Not a word until the war is over. Tell people it was too much bother, a waste of water washing it." She plucked one single strand that clung to my sleeve as if she were pulling a stitch through me. She pulled until the other end swung free, and then she placed it with the rest in the box.

And only last week with my hair all done up, I was flying. From the air, the Rockies looked flattened down. The way the shadows fell fooled me into thinking the peaks were really craters. Then the clouds piled up below, and the jet climbed to evade the weather. The Air Force had bought the seat next to me for the bomb sight. It was in its crate sitting there.

The cadets in Colorado had given it to me. An honor guard had marched across a checkerboard courtyard. And now it is home on the coffee table with the magazines, a conversation piece. It looks as if it should be potted with some viny plant, its tendrils hooking on to the knobs and buttons. Flying home after the ceremony, I wrestled it out of the box and plunked it down on my lap. It had the heft of a head, a lover gazing up at me and me stroking his hair. I leaned forward, lowering myself to the cold metal. It smelled of oil and polish. I squinted through the lens as the plane bumped beneath me, riding the turbulence over the mountains. There was just enough light, a white dime-sized hole of light. I saw the crosshairs, crisp and sharp, my dead hair, half a century old, sandwiched between the glass deep within the machine. Outside the clouds broke apart, and in the Great Basin, the lights of each tiny city lit up as the sunset fell on each of them.

And now, I have been staring at this *Redbook* spread on my lap, and my eyes won't see the words. The dryers want to lull me to sleep. From up here, the letters on the page look like the ruined walls of buildings, remains of burned foundations, blocks of pitted houses, alleyways that lead to nowhere. I follow the footprints of bombs. I was reading about hair, about its history, about its chemistry, about how we know more about it now than ever before. Below me, the words explode as I read them. One after the other. There is the roar in my ears. I sit here waiting. Soon it will be my turn again.

Pensées

THE THOUGHTS

OF

DAN QUAYLE

On the Highway of
Vice Presidents

Even from this distance, it looks like a brain. As big as an Airstream trailer and shiny like polished, dented aluminum, its skin is shrunk and crinkled, pitted and fissured.

My notes tell me it is a bioherm and that I am to blow it up, which I do. It is one of my first acts as Vice President. I am wearing a yellow hard hat when I ram down the demolition plunger as they do in action movies. The plunger makes a ripping sound like fishing line being stripped from a reel by a well-hooked bass. The engineer had told me this is the sound of an electric current being generated, *rrrrr* like a siren. We wait.

It surprised me that it took a while for the electricity I had generated to reach the charge. They had showed me the dynamite, red paper sticks bundled together with black electrician's tape. It looked like dynamite, but the fuse didn't burn like it does in cartoons. We followed the wires back to the black box where someone stripped them and attached them to the plunger by turning thumbscrews. Then another person raised a flag, a whistle blew, and a siren went off that sounded throaty and hoarse like the sound of the plunger I pushed when they said I should. We waited.

And I thought for a second about the old dinosaurs, the huge ones with long necks and long tails, and how they had walnut-sized brains and needed all these other littler brains to relay a message from the tip of the tail to the bigger brain in the head. *Hey something is biting you back here. Hey something is biting you back here. Hey something is biting you back here.* Until it got the message: *Hey something is biting me back there.*

Boom! The charge goes off. The brain-thing, which was, just the moment before, sparkling with a slick fluid of light as if it had been freshly scooped from a skull, now bursts into a brain-shaped cloud that hangs there for the longest time. Its different hemispheres bulge, contracting and squinting like it is thinking real hard. I imagine it is thinking: *What the hell happened?*

The engineer had told me that a bioherm is an ancient fossil reef built over centuries by shells of dead mollusks sinking to the floor of an ancient inland sea, cementing themselves together layer after layer. To think that Indiana was once the bottom of such a sea. I looked hard at the bioherm before we blew it up. We stood around, a group of us, having our pictures taken in front of it. I wore a yellow hard hat. I saw things that looked like snails and worms, whelk shells and mussels and clams all stuck to one another like different kinds of noodles fused together after being left in a strainer in a sink overnight. But bigger. Much bigger.

I thought about my own brain made up of all those tiny cells, each one storing the flesh of something special, a memory, say, like this one when I blew up this huge rock that wasn't a rock at all but a kind of bone sponge to make way for a highway that will bypass my hometown. I have not talked to any experts about this. It is probably the case that a brain does not work this way at all, that the cells in my head are not like ranks of offices along long corridors that account for just one scrap of information each. I shuffled through these thoughts as I thumbed through my index cards. I read a little speech then.

I remember the trucks that rumbled through Huntington, my hometown, on old 24 painted circus colors and coughing up exhaust from the stack behind the cab as they downshifted on the grade leading to the Wabash. I sat there on the hot white sidewalk and shot my hand up over my head then yanked it down and with it came the blast of the air horn from the passing truck loud enough to rattle the picture window in its frame. They liked me, I thought then, and waved. Things would happen if I made the right gestures. I could snatch the sound right out of the air, wall it away in some deep crevice in a fold of a wrinkle in my head.

Now the cloud before us in the field has lost all its glue and has turned into a gauzy curtain of sparkling powder. Through it, I see the lunky yellow earthmovers scraping along the staked out route of what will be called the Highway of Vice Presidents. The machines have a gait like crabs, their huge balloon tires stepping over the rolling floor of what my notes tell me was once an ancient inland sea.

And, later, in the Marine helicopter, my aids shouting out the briefing for the next stop of the day, we'll hover a few feet above the ground. I'll wave to the crowd gathered below. They are staggered by the blast from the prop. The dust begins to boil at their feet. The helicopter pivots on its main rotor, the long green tail lashing out and around in an arch that turns us north. I'll nod my head slightly. We'll dip forward and pick up speed, climbing. And from a distance, I'll look down as the bulldozers creep toward the scorched crater I leave behind. Huntington will be somewhere over there. With any luck I won't need to come back this way until Coats runs again for the Senate.

On the State of the Union

The Speaker bangs the gavel for order. The gavel is a gift to the United States from the people of India, the largest democracy to the world's oldest. Order.

I'm standing in front of my swivel chair next to the Speaker. I'm the President of the Senate. At the beginning of his speech the President of the United States will call me Mr. President.

The party members are still on their feet. Some are whistling, fingers stretching lips, like fans at a basketball game. The red light bounces from camera to camera around the house. The Majority are settling in, looking before they sit, picking up the text that has been distributed to their seats. Some are riffling through its pages. Others are shouting into their neighbors' ears while they continue to applaud routinely. Order.

The gavel is made of pale marble and ivory fitted with brass trim. The Speaker rests his weight on his knuckles, the gavel's handle squeezed in one fist. He looks like my father, his chin lowered, looking out at the House through his bushy brow. It makes me want to do something bad, and the boys in our party on the floor start up again after the Speaker has introduced the President just as much to see that stern mask set deeper on the Speaker's Neanderthal face as to cheer the President on.

I watch the red light on the cameras as it goes off and on around the room. I try to guess where it will alight next. The one in the lobby doorway. The one fixed on the mezzanine wall. The one behind the Speaker that shows the fanned seating of the floor. The angle that captures the various Secretaries and Generals and Ambassadors. I never know when the camera will focus on me. I am looking thoughtful, I think, as I applaud. The light flickers on the camera aimed at the wives in the gallery above. I follow the vector from that camera, its lens slowly extending for a tight close-up on the First Lady, who stands by the railing in the blue dress with big buttons, pearls bubbling at her throat, her eyes glassy, as always, applauding effortlessly. I see her over the President's right shoulder, smoothing her skirt around her hips as she sits down. And we all sit down.

Her husband begins to speak, and I remind myself to count the number of times he will be interrupted by applause. I know the words that are cues. The Whips have briefed us in caucus. There are plants salted in the gallery to trigger responses. The pauses are scripted. I always tell myself that I will keep track of the applause to match the number with the talking heads at the networks. But I lose track. My thoughts flit away from me like that light that now burns on the camera in the center aisle below us suddenly extinguishing itself and suddenly flaring up again after completing a circuit of the room during an interlude of cheering.

They've been working on the President. I can see the line of Pan-Cake on his neck where the napkin masked his white collar. Color has been brushed on the cheek he turns toward me when his head scans the room. His hair is freshly dyed, the television lights polishing the contours, each strand lacquered into place.

I know what people are thinking. They see me brooding behind the President. I have touched up my own temples with a hint of gray. It is important that we all forget about the President's mortality. I alone am allowed to age. I imagine the Members on the floor squirming in their seats, adjusting their angles of vision, using the bulk of the President to blot me and then the thought of me out of their minds. The President's most recent collapse, captured on television, has brought me back into their thoughts that now are drifting away from the prepared text, the paragraph on infrastructure they have been following halfheartedly, and into that percentage of every minute each has allotted to daydream, fantasy, or prayer. I walk in the corridors of some skulls out there. The possibility of me. The blue-eyed, bushy-tailed fact of me.

To get back at them, I employ the old Toastmaster trick of imagining the audience naked, and they sit there like dollops of frosting, their famous gray heads collapsing into puddles of fat that fill the seats. The esteemed colleague from Rhode Island is a smear of freckles. There, Howie has a rash that itches. I see secret tattoos. Trickles of sweat deliberately trace the topography of Teddy's sagging breast. The thighs, worn smooth, shiny, and white by a life dedicated to always wearing trousers, straddle the shriveled assortment of penises, the Members' members, that now are listening to their owners' own state of the union, a message of hope and resurrection punctuated by a worn catalog of past and very private images. Order. Order.

Up on the toes of their naked feet, cheering, their flesh jiggles and sways, breaks out in splotches of color. Bill's thighs have been stripped of veins for his bypass. The gentleman from New Jersey has new plugs. They are otherwise unremarkable, marked only for the death they have convinced themselves for now does not exist for them. The cancer ticks in a chest, a strangled heart, a brain that forgets to remember. There is another nakedness beneath the twill layer of beige skin. And it is, perhaps, only accessible to me from my strange vantage on this dais looking out at them all. I see into them. My job description gives me this vision since all I do is wait on death. I am the official mourner. The shadow of death cast a few polite paces behind the aging President.

Above us all, the First Lady, also naked, her face framed by an aurora of hair, rises from her seat and continues to rise to hover near the ceiling. A gesture of etched lines divides her body into hemispheres of breasts and belly and clefts of her butt, a kind of ancient statue, veined marble and ivory. She cleaves apart suddenly. The parts whirling into a system of orbiting planets. The President looks up at the glowing constellation of his wife.

The President's speech continues. All of it has already been distributed. It is being delivered as if by a machine. I witness the essential part of him leave himself for a moment, shedding the shell of his suit, to float up above the august chamber of the House of Representatives, joining the animated and precious flesh of his wife.

I think such thoughts because the President thinks such thoughts. Much of what we do is fantasy. It is my job to dream his dreams. In case he is unable to complete his constitutional duties, I am ready to step into his place.

I chair, at the pleasure of the President, a commission on space. I see in his dark suit the deep black fabric of the universe. There are still flakes of white dandruff on the shoulders and back. I stare into the depths between those flecks of white transforming into twinkling stars. It is a map of heavenly bodies. This vacuum has a texture. I lose my way in its blackness. I no longer hear the speech. On television, I will appear lost in grave thought. I have forgotten the spontaneous applause. The infinite silence between those stars terrifies me.

On the Tomb of
the Unknown Soldier

Who were these soldiers? The hairless living ones who helped me place the wreath at the Tomb of the Unknown Soldier. One of them was black. One was white. But what I saw of what was left of their faces (the glossy brims of their caps squashed down on their noses and the straps hid the lips outlining the metallic exterior jaws) were identical grim expressions made up of the least expressive parts, the plane geometry of their cheeks and chins. Their hands were gloved and gripped the green florist's wire stand that connected them as if it ran out of their palms and extruded through their squeezing fingers. Their skeletons must have been made of the same pinched wire running through the clay. When they moved, they moved only the moving part. Marching, the legs didn't disturb the head or torso. When they lifted the flowers, their hands alone snatched them up. Their wrists ratcheted to a predetermined calibration in the joints. A pause and then their heads snapped forward together, leaving their bodies still facing the wreath they held motionless between them. Another pause, then their left legs stepped toward the tomb, Egyptian, the mechanism of the hips hidden beneath the flare of their blue belted jackets. The air reeked of carnations and roses and mothballs that had steeped their wool uniforms. I followed them conscious of the wobble in my limbs, my wrinkled suit, my puckered face, my hair blowing into my eyes.

As a congressman, I had sent visiting constituents out to Arlington to see the show, shaking their hands at the door of the hired cab. Sometimes, I went myself and took the kids if they were out of school in time to watch the changing of the guard. I counted the twenty-one gliding steps along the red carpet, the twenty-one seconds of silence between the pivots and the echoing heel clicks, the twenty-one steps back past the tomb. Suddenly the replacement and an officer would appear, enter into the rhythm. They barked at each other. The officer inspected the rifles. His hands breaking open the breech. His head snapping his chin to his chest as he looked from behind his dark aviator glasses at the gleaming round in the exposed chamber. Twenty-one steps. Twenty-one seconds. The officer and relieved soldier slid off the runway when the new guard stopped to click his heels. They disappeared behind the cedar trees that screen the barracks.

My grandmother took the copper bracelet she wore in memory of the missing Navy flier of the Vietnam War with her to her grave. I remember reading the name and dates on the green band around her wrist as the family removed the other jewelry before the casket was closed. We decided to leave it on since he'd never been found and because my grandmother always said the copper helped with her arthritis. We left the hearing aid in her ear as well, her plates. The pacemaker was buried in her chest. She had an artificial hip of titanium and gold made by a company in Warsaw, Indiana, in my old district. It is guaranteed to survive forever.

I saluted as the soldiers placed the flowers before the tomb. Beneath the slabs of marble at my feet there were remains of unknown American soldiers from the other wars that followed. World War II and Korea. We have gotten better at knowing though. There is a marker for the Vietnam War, but nobody from that war is unknown really, everyone has been accounted for. Everyone is alive, dead, or missing. Say a tooth turns up in a riddle sifting the dirt from a crash site in a Delta paddy. It is rushed to the lab in Hawaii, and they puzzle it out and match the tooth with a name. The classifications shift. There is nothing left to find in the jungle that will now leave us ignorant. You are either lost or found. But not unknown.

So just what is interred here? Perhaps we've created a Gothic monster in reverse, not animated after being stitched together from pilfered corpses, but a fake pile of remains constructed out of the stolen wax limbs of movie monsters posing in Hollywood museums. What is buried here is still known only to God; it just isn't human. The only part of it that is human at all is the lie that placed an empty coffin here, that sustains the fiction. We buried a symbol. We buried not knowing. Be we know. We know we know.

In Disneyland they maintain a Hall of Presidents, a stage filled with jerking dummies of the dead Commanders in

Chief. After I'm dead, if all has gone right, something that looks like me will nod its head sagely seated next to the smiling hulks of Lincoln and Hoover. The engineers have worked so hard to encode grace and gesture into my lower right arm. They move from tendon to muscle and back again, experiment with a new substance more like cartilage, import artificial femurs and rotor cuffs from the factory in Warsaw, Indiana. Programs to scratch an ear run for thousands of pages.

On this other stage, these living boys of The President's Own Guard, having practiced alone in their barracks, wish to extinguish every twitch. They force themselves not to blink. They wire their jaws shut with will. They attach governors to their stride, unlearning their bodies. Who are they? As taps played, I concentrated, trying to catch one of them breathing. I could hear in the silence between the sad notes only the whirr of the cameras winding after the hiss of the shutters.

Before all this pomp, between the world wars, families came to the cemetery and used the marble tomb as a table for picnics. They looked out over the new sod of a field of Civil War dead. The place was only occasionally guarded then by groups of veterans who would police the area for the scored wax paper, the chicken bones, and the child's ball left behind. Who knows? Perhaps it was a better ceremony to stretch out on the marble table after a big dinner and let the sun feast on your itching skin. Perhaps better than a wreath. Watching the unflinching bodies of the soldiers at attention, I imagined losing myself. I was a statue come to life, tap-dancing on the plinth of the Unknown Soldier, looking out over the Potomac to the distant white memorials melting in the haze.

The crowd of people assembled for that Memorial Day applauded as I walked away. They know who I am, they think. I let them think what they think.

On Late-Night TV

The television is secondhand from the White House, an early color model dating from the Johnson administration. The mahogany cabinet, gaudy as a casket, holds three screens. I can tune each to a different channel, watch the same network on all three. It has been modified for remote. It is cable ready, and three VCRs have been hooked up. Johnson had it built so he could watch simultaneously the three versions of the evening news. The maps of Vietnam were in different colors. He must have had an aide at the ready, turning the volume controls by hand. "Let me hear Cronkite, the bastard," he would bark. Or maybe he just left on all the sound. He would have to distinguish who said what the way you pick out instruments in a symphony. I can see him, slouched in a swivel chair, his tie loosened, his eyes skipping from screen to screen to screen, the room filled with the babbling voices. I watched the same war on WISH-TV in Indianapolis never dreaming that it would come out like this.

Most of the furniture we have here at the old Naval Observatory was once in the White House. Each new resident sweeping clean, sends tables and chairs, portraits and drapes, mantel clocks and mirrors over in the GSA vans. The first floor looks like a furniture showroom. The televisions, however, I had sent up to our room. In the evenings, propped up in the water bed we brought with us to Washington, I watch the televisions. The mattress is slightly baffled to dampen the waves. Still, it is soothing, the gentle rocking. I float, watching the late-night shows.

Marilyn falls asleep each night after the local weather. Curled away from me under the light blanket, she wears a frilly black blindfold like the ones panelists wore on old game shows. The elastic band bunches her hair together into a dark helmet. She snores politely beside me. The sheets are silk. There is a slight roll in the mattress. The polyester in the blanket will discharge static from time to time, faint sparks tracing her hair and shoulders, letting me know she is here.

On the far wall, the televisions are on. The screens seem to float too, a slight flicker in the pictures. I like to arrange the programs from left to right. I have a remote in each hand, and I am good enough now to read the buttons with my thumbs like braille. I can start with Carson on the first screen, then move to Arsenio in the middle. While I am watching him, noting the strange new design cut into his hair, I can leapfrog Johnny's image to the screen on the right, catching him as he turns toward Doc. My fingers are busy moving Arsenio from the middle screen left, nudging the volume up there so that I can hear his first joke while I watch Carson, arms behind his back, lean forward toward the audience like a figure on a ship's prow. I cue up Ted Koppel on the middle set just to find out tonight's subject. If I'm not interested, I'll switch to the comedy channel with its parade of club stand-ups or run the tape of the morning talk shows, scanning for any reference to me until it is time for Dennis Miller to come on after *Nightline* on ABC.

If I am alert enough, I can record the jokes on the other two VCRs. I now sense when a joke is coming. When Leno stands in for Johnny, he uses me last after a string of gags based on the day's headlines. He likes to end with me. Arsenio seems embarrassed, the punch line swallowed, buried in his nervous guffaw. It is almost as if he feels compelled to make a joke about me. I am able to catch a couple of these jokes a night, save them on one of the two 120-minute cassettes.

Late at night, after all the talk shows are over and the overnight news shows are on the networks, I'll run the tape, one long string of jokes about me. I want to remember who said what. There are the nightly bits that turn on my stupidity, and then the frenzy of jokes when I have done or said something silly. "Did you see where our vice president visited Los Angeles?" The comic shakes his head. "This is true," he says. "He had a few things to say about television." The audience is already howling. He goes on with the joke. Quiet, I think, I want to hear this. I want to know what's true, you bastard. Tell me what's true.

On the other screens, I like to run the weather channels, with their shifts of nameless hosts pointing at loops of computer-enhanced weather swirling left to right across the map of the nation. The comic appears between two computer-enhanced maps of the country. The storm warnings are boxed out, the line of storms a slash of red.

Weatherpeople look like ordinary people. Rumpled and tired. Their suits are off the rack. Their jokes are corny, harmless. I like to watch the weather dancing behind them. I know it isn't actually there but projected on the screen, blended into the signal by the control room mixers. The screen they point to is really blank, and they must look at a monitor offstage to see the map. They learn to do this by watching television. I could watch them do this for hours.

While I was in law school, I did watch David Letterman do the weather on that Indianapolis station, sticking pictures of umbrellas and smiling suns in sunglasses on an airbrushed map of Indiana. He drew arrows that meant nothing, made up forecasts on the spot, and teased the anchors, who smiled back at him. The other students thought he was funny. My study group took a break to watch him every night. He would spend his time asking on the air what a flurry was, who had seen high pressure, why was Indiana always colored pink.

And now I have him on all three screens. He fiddles with his suit, licks his teeth, presses his face into the camera. His jokes aren't funny, and the audience doesn't laugh. But the funny part is, I think, that that is what is supposed to happen. The audience groans and boos. The harder he works, the more it fails, the better the audience likes it. I don't get this being dumb. I don't get it.

At 2:00 A.M. the dogs in Washington start barking. I can hear sirens going up and down Massachusetts Avenue. I have been watching the weather. There will be snow in Vail and sunshine in Palm Beach. It's a great country. You can ski or play golf on the same day. I've been watching a show-length commercial for a new kind of paintbrush and, on several channels, the pictures of the pouting women who say they will talk with me live if I call them right now.

All the phone traffic is logged here at the residency. I couldn't get away with dialing a 900 number. There would be a leak. Word would get out. I can anticipate the jokes late at night, the winks. I can almost make them up myself.

Marilyn snores, and her snoring sets up a rocking in the bed. The water sloshes. She rolls over, and her face turns toward me. Her eyes are masked, but I can see the twinkling blue screens reflected deep within the black satin.

I want to walk onto *The Tonight Show* in the middle of someone's time in the guest chair the way Bob Hope does. Perhaps on Carson's very last show. I want to straighten this whole thing out. Let people see me as I really am.

"I can only stay a minute, Johnny," I'd say. He apologizes for that evening's joke during the monologue. "Hey, I understand. I'm used to it." I can take it. I'd show them.

I watch the televisions. I start with the one on the left. The later it gets, the more ads there are for private conversations. The women say they are standing by, waiting for the phones to ring. I could call right now. I could. I would tell them who I am. And they believe me right away. I say, "I'm the Vice President." I say, "No, really. I'm not making this up. I am the Vice President. I am. I am."

On Anesthesia

The naval officer with the football clutches it like, well, a football, tucked under one arm and the other arm wrapped over the top. We call it the football, but it's not a football. It's a silver briefcase stuffed with all the secret codes for launching the missiles and the bombers. He slumps in his chair at the far end of the Oval Office. Secret Service agents, packed into the couches, read old *People* magazines. The lenses of their dark glasses lighten automatically the longer they're inside. They've let me sit at the President's desk in the big leather swivel chair. Now my back is to them. I'm looking out at the Rose Garden, where the white buckets weighted down with bricks protect the plants. On the bureau beneath the window, the President has a ton of pictures. His kids and grandkids. His brothers and sisters. Shots of Christmases. The house in Maine. His wife. The dog. I don't see me. Little elephants are scattered among the frames. Carved in stone or wood or cast in polished metal, they all head the same direction, their trunks raised and trumpeting.

Every few minutes I like to turn dramatically around to

face the room. Nothing happens. The agents flip through the magazines, licking their thumbs to turn the pages. Other aides huddle by the door fingering each other's lapel pins. The naval officer with the football has a rag out now. He breathes on the briefcase, then rubs the fog off the shiny surface.

I get to be President for about twenty minutes more. The real President is under anesthesia at Bethesda. In the big cabinet room the chiefs of staff are watching the operation on a closed-circuit hookup. A stenographer is taking down everything that's being said. They asked me if I wanted to watch with them, but I get squeamish at the sight of blood. I'd wait in the Oval Office I told them. An amendment to the Constitution lets me be Acting President in such situations, but there is nothing for me to do. We've been ignoring the press. No sense mentioning it.

I've been doodling on White House stationery I found in the desk drawer. I always draw parallel zigzagging lines, connecting them up to form steps. When I am finished I can look at the steps the regular way and then I can make myself see them upside down, flipping back and forth in my head from one way to the other. I arrange the pens on the desk blotter after I've used them as if I am going to give them out as souvenirs.

They let me make a few phone calls. I called a supporter in Phoenix, but I forgot about the time difference and I woke him up. What could I say? I'm sorry. I left a message for the Governor of Indiana, a Democrat I play golf with sometimes. His father, when he was a Senator, wrote the amendment that let me be President for a few hours. "Just tell him the President called," I said. I wanted to rub it in. I called Janine, my high school girlfriend, who is an actuary in Chicago. I don't know her politics. "Guess where I am," I said. She couldn't guess. When I traveled commercial I used to call her at her home from O'Hare on a stopover. I let her know I was a Congressman, a Senator. I wanted her to know I was on my way someplace.

"Try," I said. "From where I sit I can see the Washington Memorial." That wasn't true. I was looking at the Commander with the football. She told me she was running late, that her eggs were getting cold. Janine had a view of the lake, I imagined, her building near a beach on the North Shore.

"I've got to go," I said. "This is on the taxpayers' nickel." I wanted everyone to hear me. The men in the room, I could see, were trying hard not to look like they were listening.

I was anesthetized once. This was a few years ago. All four of my wisdom teeth were impacted. Before they put me under, I had to read a form and sign it. It said I understood all the things that could go wrong. The procedure was usually performed on patients much younger. Nerves could get cut. Dry sockets. Shattered jawbones. I don't like blood or guts, so I signed it quickly to stop thinking about the possibilities. I signed, sitting in the chair while the oral surgeon held up the syringe, squirting out drops of the drug from the gleaming needle.

"We are going to put you into twilight sleep," the doctor told me. "Not really sleep. Not deep enough to dream. You'll just be very relaxed," he said, slapping at my arm to find a vein. "If we weren't going to work in your mouth, you'd tell us all your secrets. You'd just let go."

I was out like a light. It felt like sleeping in a seat on an airplane. I remember thinking I wish I knew what my secrets were, what I really thought. But the drug that made me tell the truth also put me into twilight sleep so that I never really knew what I said. I know I was talking, telling them everything. I kept rocking along through the dark night. Then, the doctor and the nurses were looking at me strangely. Had they heard me say something, the muttering I had been making becoming clear when they swabbed up the blood or turned away to pick up another instrument? Did they stop and listen?

Tell me what I said, I said to them. But it came out nonsense. I could just begin to feel my face again, feel it swelling up. My lips and tongue had vanished.

"Who stole my tongue?" I said.

"Is someone coming to drive you home?" they asked as they walked me into another room.

"Ma mamph," I said. I could hear again. I was vaguely aware of other bodies on cots scattered around the room. The doctor and the nurse eased me onto my own cot. They stuck a sheet of instructions in my hands and slid a small envelope into my shirt pocket.

"Those are your teeth," they said. I had wanted to do something with the molars, polish them up and have them made into jewelry or shellac them for a paperweight. But when I opened the envelope later all that spilled out were splinters of bone, crumbs of teeth. They had to be chiseled out the doctor told me when I called. "They didn't want to budge," he said.

I looked at the pile of fragments on my desk. Here and there I could see a smooth contour of a tooth, the tip of a root, the sliced off crown like a flat-bottomed cloud. I pushed the parts around on the desk. Most were ragged, caked with clotted blood and bits of browning tissue. The pulpy nerves crumpled to dust. I poked the pieces into four piles, the bits making a scratching sound as they slid across the stationery they were on. I had drawn stairs on the paper, and I climbed them up and down, up and down.

Maybe it was the painkiller I was still taking. I sat there staring at the piles of dust thinking: These are all my secrets reduced to ashes.

"It's the drugs," Marilyn said when I told her how sad my wisdom teeth had made me. I tried to explain that the operation had pried something out of me. I couldn't begin to explain it. "It's the drugs talking," she said.

The kitchen timer the Secret Service set bings on the end table, and they all stand up from the couches. They toss the *People* magazines in a heap on the coffee table. I turn back to the window and see the naval officer sprinting for the helicopter revving up on the lawn. He'll fly directly to Bethesda. The official White House photographer snaps a few pictures of me at the desk. A Secret Service agent rushes my doodles to the shredder in the closet. "You want me to dial the phone," I ask, "sign a few papers? What?"

"Just act natural," the photographer says as aides usher Marilyn into the room. I stand up, push the chair from the desk. We kiss in front of the bureau, the elephants sniffing up at us. I hear the snap, snap of the camera, sense the white flash on my eyelids.

I am sentimental, I think. I feel lots of things. I just don't let anyone know. No one will know how it felt to be the President of the United States for a few hours. Janine, on her way to work, cannot begin to imagine the depth of my feelings. Everyone else, the whole country waking up and getting ready for the new day, they can't begin to imagine what I feel I feel.

The photographer wants another picture of us kissing. Marilyn leans into me again, her eyes closed, her head cocked to the right. I could kiss her on the cheek or on her mouth. Kissing is all different now. After the extraction of my teeth I found that feeling would never return to my lips, the nerve endings crushed or severed by the operation. I don't like to think about that, nerves and tissues. I decide to kiss her mouth, and I do. It is a sensation I've grown to like. The numbness.

On Barbie

"What is your real name?" I ask the woman who is Barbie. She is shivering next to me as we stand in the open doorway at the end of the assembly line. The satin sash she wears matches the ribbon we are supposed to cut. The sky is gray, and the pigeons, scared up by the band music, are spiraling back down to the holes in the eaves and windows of the unused part of the factory where they roost. She tells me her name as she takes my arm. Her hard hat floats on top of her thick hair.

"You could be Ken," she whispers to me. "Let's pretend."

The CEO and owner of this plant is speaking to a crowd of workers and reporters who spill out to the big parking lot. I've thought of that. I could be Ken. I have that block-shaped head. The hairline and the line of the jaw are Ken's. I smile at her, imagining the way we look. I am holding the giant pair of scissors with my other hand. Barbie and Ken and a pair of scissors scaled to make us look doll-sized. Our smiles are frozen on our faces. You have to practice this. Yes, I could be Ken. He's a good-looking guy. I take it as a compliment.

The Corvettes spaced along the line are pink. This factory now makes all kinds of electric cars for kids. The cars have two forward speeds and one in reverse controlled by pedals and gearshifts. The detailing of the paint and upholstery matches the vehicle it is modeled on. But I am told it is the novelty of the keys that come with the car, starting it up and shutting it off, that sells the product. Children in elementary school love them. They carry their jingling key rings to class for show-and-tell.

"It is like a real car," the CEO told me earlier. The Corvettes are just one line called Barbie's Corvette. It's a licensing agreement with Mattel. "And it comes in any color you want," the CEO said, "as long as it is pink."

I thought it was a bad idea driving one of the Corvettes around the parking lot. The CEO and the PR people had hoped I would take one for a spin. I thought of Dukakis in the tank. I pictured myself wedged in the tiny cockpit, my knees up by my ears, my hands on the steering wheel between my feet. The Secret Service were to act as pylons. Stiff as posts, staring from behind their dark glasses at everything except me. I would scoot around their legs in the car, turning a complete circle around one agent, then slalom back through their dispersed pattern on the parking lot, a test track. I would try to cut the corners as close as possible, trench coats slapping my face.

Instead of driving one of the cars, I admired them during a photo opportunity. One turned slowly on a tabletop turntable, the television lights playing over its pink gloss finish. Barbie stroked the fenders with the fingers of her long hand. This was my first look at the car. The ribbon-cutting ceremony at the end of the assembly line came later. We were to take a tour of the plant and the factory showroom, where salesmen walked among the highly polished demonstration models handing out brochures. When we got there, we picked our way through the cars at our feet, the miniature Mercedes and tiny Jeeps. We stopped to marvel at a replica of a '57 T-bird coupe.

"Oh," Barbie said bending over to pet it, "so cute."

This is what Vice Presidents do. Bury the dead and open factories. This factory had once made tractors for semi-trailers, Trans Stars for the local van line company, and green Army two-and-a-halfs. The white star stenciled on the door. The factory is in Fort Wayne, in my home district. It had been a ruin for ten years, ever since Harvester closed the plant in favor of one in Springfield, Missouri.

When I was a kid, my father brought me up here. He was covering a rollout for the paper then. Crammed onto a reviewing stand, we watched the trucks blast around the banked track, stutter over a patch of cobblestones, then plow through a shallow pool splaying a wake of water from beneath each wheel. I got to climb up in the cab as the engine idled and rumbled beneath the seat. With my arms stretched wide I couldn't hold both sides of the steering wheel.

On the way back to Huntington, my father tried to explain the future to me. The truck I had been in was just an idea, its model year two or three years away. I didn't get it. I had smelled the diesel fumes, heard the sneeze of the air brakes. "Who know," my father said, "a lot could happen."

I let them love me in Fort Wayne. I swung a grant their way. Jawboned the locals for tax relief. Some people are working again. Let them blame that on me.

"I am really Malibu Barbie," Barbie says to me. "The doll comes with a Frisbee, a tote bag, and a beach umbrella." That is why she is wearing the swimsuit on this early spring day. The sky is as dirty as the grime on the big windows. Off in the distance, at the other end of the property, is the red brick bell tower. The old company logo, the small *i* bisecting the capital *H* to look like a gearshift pattern, still hangs crookedly just beneath the roof. The stink of the drawn copper from the wire works next door begins to coat my tongue.

"You from around here?" I ask her. Her neck is long and thin. Her swimsuit is made out of a miracle fabric in an animal hide print. She is wearing sheer hose that sparkle even in the bad light and hiss like scissor blades cutting construction paper when she walks.

Earlier, we toured the whole factory, even the abandoned parts. The new assembly line took up a fraction of the acres under roof. The toy car company had been started in the owner's garage. At first he just made go-carts for the neighborhood kids. Then, as business grew, he moved to a Quonset hut in an industrial park. There is plenty of room to expand now.

Barbie's heels snipped over the steel plate on the floor

that had covered the conduits for cables that fed the old machines long removed. On the terrazzo I could see where they had been positioned from the footprints of discolored flooring outlined with filth. Here and there were rusting heaps of metal that could not be salvaged and yellowing scraps of paper that looked like scaling fungus on rotting trees. The factory opened up to three stories, the web of girders supporting the roof lost in the gloom. Dripping water from somewhere matched Barbie's cadence. We stopped in the middle of the vast hall to rest. There was a little oasis of gunmetal stools and desk chairs on coasters. The Secret Service drifted on, their backs to us, spreading apart to form a perimeter, right on the edge of being seen. No one spoke. What light there was seemed to be drawn to Barbie, who swiveled slowly in the office chair. Her legs, crossed at the ankles, stretched out to keep her pointed feet off the floor. Her head was thrown back, the hard hat adhering to her hair. She closed her eyes as if she were sunbathing. She shimmered, bobbing like a needle in a toy compass slowly nudging north. I could hear the pigeons cooing in the rafters and then suddenly flapping after launching out, gliding into sight to land on the floor across the room.

"You know," I said to Barbie, "we always live in the age of lead. We stand on the shoulders of giants." I looked at her to see what impression I had made.

"Oh, I know," she said. "Look at the toys these days. Nothing is left to the imagination."

I felt like an accessory in a new play set. Call it Barbie's

Factory. Action figures and clothes sold separately. Any moment the vast roof could crack open, the walls hinging out. I am Midwestern Ken. A seed cap, dungarees, and a farmer's tan.

Barbie is a head taller than I am. I sat quietly and watched her turn in the chair, propelled by invisible forces. The Secret Service whispered to each other in the shadows.

At the end of the day, we cut the ribbon. I grasp one handle with both my hands. Barbie has the other. I remember again the gigantic wheel of the truck. I am confused, confused again by size. I never fit. I never fit no matter what I do. The scissors are useless at cutting through the ribbon, the fabric folding then slipping between the blades. We end up tearing through it after the threads of the edge have been frayed enough by our frantic efforts. We pull the handles apart, then hurl them back together. The blades slicing closed smack with a kiss.

Barbie leans over and gives me a kiss. Her lips are waxy on my cheek. We pose that way. Barbie's long neck stretched out as she nuzzles my face. A hand on each of my shoulders for support. I am smiling at the cameras. This is what I am thinking. I'm thinking: It's a small moment of triumph no matter how you look at it.

The air is permeated with the tang of metal. I hold out in front of me the shiny keys that fit the brand-new pink Barbie Corvette I was given, which the Secret Service will later carry out to my limousine and store in the trunk like a spare to begin our trip back to Washington. And later still, in an intimate ceremony on the Mall, I will donate the car to the

Smithsonian. Mattel will send another Barbie, this one dressed in a gold gown that might have been worn at an inaugural. Together, with the pink car roped off in one corner of the museum, we will have staked out our own little piece of history.

On Hoosier Hysteria

This is true. During the annual high school basketball tournaments in Indiana, the winning small towns send a team to the cities for the regional or semistate finals. Those towns empty completely for the games, the whole population evacuated by yellow buses and strings of private sedans and wagons. The Governor declares an emergency and sends a few state troopers or a truckload of the Guard to patrol the deserted streets.

I got sent to Marion one spring when that team was playing up in Fort Wayne. I was attached to a clerical unit stationed at Fort Benjamin Harrison outside of Indianapolis. We convoyed up from the south and parked on the outskirts of the ville as the residents streamed north. We could hear the horns. A muscle car sped by camouflaged with crepe paper and tempera. We were humping it into town, two files, one to a gutter, along the main street. The lieutenant sent a squad down a side street. Dogs barked. Up ahead was the small downtown of two-storied stores and offices. Hovering just above the brick buildings, a huge water tower seemed to float like a dark cloud, its supporting legs obscured by the buildings and trees. There was writing on its side that couldn't be read from where I was, the town name and zip code perhaps, the sense of it stretched around out of sight. We had to hold the town for the day, and, if the team won its afternoon game, stay the night in bivouac set up on the high school football field.

It took us a few hours or so to walk the streets and rattle some door handles. Tacked up on every garage was a scuffed backboard and rotting net. I looked in the windows of the empty homes, saw the big glossy house and garden magazines scalloped on the coffee table, the dishrag draped over the faucet in the kitchen, an old pitcher filled with pussy willow branches in the middle of the dining table. Some places were unlocked, and I poked my head in, shouting to make sure no one was there. As I walked through one house, I listened to the clocks ticking. There was Eckrich meat in the refrigerator. I turned on the television and stood in front of it as it warmed up. The game was on, live, the boys going through warm-up drills at each end of the court. Somewhere in the crowd, the people who lived in that house shook pom-poms behind the cheerleaders. I stood there, too close to the set, in the living room, in full gear, my helmet on my head, cradling my rifle in my arms. The boys in their shiny outfits did layup after layup. Each of them took a little skip as he started to break for the hoop, meeting the feeding pass in midstride, the ball then rolling off his fingers, kissing the glass. A sergeant tapped on the picture window. "Quayle," he said, his voice filtering into the house, "get your butt out here."

I followed a squad down an oiled street. The sidewalks had crumbled into dust. The Kiwanis had tapped the maple trees growing along the side of the road, the sap plunking inside the tin buckets. We formed up at the end of the block, where the town met the surrounding field of corn stubble. The field went on for miles, broken only by a stand of trees, a cluster of buildings, a cloud of crows rising from the ground. We stood there waiting for something to happen. How strange and empty the world had become. In a few more weeks spring would be here for good, but you would never guess it from the way things looked. It was as if we had survived something horrible. I felt frightened and relieved. Then, the sergeant told us to saddle up and get back to town.

Later, we watched the game on a television we brought with us from the armory. The little diesel generator sputtered outside the tent. Marion won and would play again that night. We ate K rations while we watched, fruit salad in Army green tins. I saved the cherries for the last after eating the peaches, the pears, the pineapple, and the grapes in that order.

And later still, I climbed the water tower and circled the tank on the wire catwalk, looking down on the town. I saw the grid of streetlights come on automatically in patches down below. A sentry in one neighborhood waded through the puddles of light. A truck or a car would rumble up the main street and brake at the checkpoint near the square. On the wall of the water tank, high school kids had scratched their initials in the paint, coupling them with the stitch of plus signs. Now I was too close to read the huge letters of the town name and the legend that declared Marion was the Home of the Little Giants and the numbers of the years they had won the state championship. You had to read that from the ground. In my pocket was a souvenir I'd pilfered from a house below, a gravy boat from a corner cupboard. I have it still.

And when Marion won the game that night, I could hear the troops shouting that the home team had won. I watched from the platform on the water tower as all the patrolling soldiers came running from their posts to see the team cut down the nets on TV. From my perch, I looked north to the haze of light where Fort Wayne was supposed to be, re-creating in my own mind the whole celebration I knew by heart.

I was floating above a peaceful Indiana in the dark. Out there, there were winners and losers. After tonight, we'd be down to the final four. I thought then, and I think now, that this is what we were fighting for.

On 911

He used to walk everywhere, Ed, the incumbent I beat for the congressional seat that got me to Washington. His campaign consisted of taking walks. He'd walk through a neighborhood in Fort Wayne, going up and knocking on a few doors, waving at cars as they passed by him. He gave out stickers in the shape of footprints and in the outline of shoes. He'd walk out into the country, out to Zulu and Avilla, Markle and Noblesville. The few reporters that trailed along tired after a few miles, caught a ride back downtown. He was a tall thin man. He slung his jacket over his shoulder, his shirtsleeves rolled up to his elbows. His pants were too short. Along Indiana 3, he'd wade through the patches of wild carrot and goldenrod. He was bombed by the angry blackbirds. He had thin hair and wore glasses with clear plastic frames. Near Leo, the Amish, who don't even vote, passed him by in their buggies. He would stop at a farmhouse for a drink of water from a well. He'd get his picture in *The Journal,* the Democratic paper, kicking an empty can along the gutter in the streets of the new suburbs of St. Joe Township. He was always alone, hardly talked to anyone that mattered. No one walked anymore. His shoes were always dusty. It was a cinch.

After I won and Ed was showing me around the Hill, he refused to ride the Capitol subway over to his office. He put me onboard, and we left him behind to walk over by himself. His aides even rode with me. They didn't bother looking back to see him shrink in the poor light of the dark tunnel beneath the streets of Washington.

He was too pitiful for words. He had more than enough rope to hang himself. The few rumors we fanned at Rotary clubs and the Zonta were enough. His skin was milky. His voice was pitched too high. He smoked a pipe. The pictures you saw in *The Journal* always showed him from behind, the loose white shirt draped with that summer-weight jacket. Such a target, his back exposed, brought the best out of the voters. I salivated along with my staff as we watched him walk through the fall.

His one piece of legislation was the bill that established an emergency telephone number, 911. Something a child could remember and dial. I can just imagine the debate. Who would oppose it? What could be wrong with it?

I imagine him right now sitting in his rec room watching television, perhaps the show that dramatizes the rescues once someone has called the emergency number. Every time I watch that program, I think of him in his recliner, feeling good about his public life, the stories he watches a kind of endless testimonial to his goodness.

When I was a kid, I believed in creating a kind of chronic discomfort, using the telephone to disrupt the workaday world. "Do you have Prince Edward in the can? You do? Well, you better let him out." I dialed the numbers randomly. "Is your refrigerator running? It is? Well, you better go chase it." I flipped through the phone book looking for funny names, calling the Frankensteins or the Cockburns. I liked transforming the telephone into something dangerous. People being startled by the bell, their hands frozen for a moment before reaching the rest of the way to pick up. My little voice, a needle in their ears, creating these anxious moments. Let him out! Go chase it! I'd make up fictions to clear the party line so that I could call my girlfriend. Or I would listen to the neighbors talking to each other, letting them know I was there. I would always be there.

A guy like you, Ed, would keep on answering the phone, would think after all the heavy breathing I'd want to talk with you. You believe in signs, in what they say. The tinkling bells of the ice cream truck would have you racing down the street. You answer the phone without a second thought. Is your refrigerator running?

Poor Ed. Everything in the world can be used, used in ways you'd never dream, used against you. Twisted. Devoured. Pulled inside out. I like to imagine you cringing in your dark rec room, the flicker of your television slapping you around, your sweaty skin sticking to the gummy vinyl of your lounger. I made you crawl. You were so easy to kick. I watched you drag yourself along the oiled back roads, the uncut ditches of Allen County, where well-bred children who hurl rocks at the Amish buggies just to hear the wood splinter took aim at you.

In the bedrooms of America, no one ever entertains the fantasy of a liberal with a whip. They desire something more, something more like me but dressed to the hilt in black uniform and patent leather, professional looking, someone who might be truly dangerous. It's in the eyes. It's there in the tight smile. In the privacy of their own rec rooms some people like to dress up. People like to be hurt. People like to hurt. They play out their own amateur versions of epic conflicts. Here words don't mean the same things. Saying stop doesn't work. Stop means keep on going. Try to imagine it. What to yell when things get out of hand, when the stimulation in these dramas exceeds the threshold of endurance? I've heard they scream or mutter: 911. 911. The number you invented has been absorbed into this language of love.

I hate to think about these things at all. But we live in the sickest of times. It's still a matter of trust. Your partner will stop if you find the right thing to say. What can I say, Ed? What number can I call? It seems I can't exist without these dramas. There are the good guys and the bad guys. I like that. Someone gets hurt. Someone does the hurting. And the bells keep ringing.

On *Quayleito*

I know now how it works. I spent one afternoon in my office with an eyeglasses repair kit dismantling the thing. I unscrewed the little screws that held the tiny hinges, unhooked the rubber bands, untied the threads with tweezers, freed the minute springs as fine as hair. The pieces lay scattered on my desk blotter. I put the various parts in the empty squares of days mapped out on the appointment calendar. I had been ordered to lay low awhile, rehabilitate myself.

I never drink the water anywhere. It can make you sick. But in Chile, I waded into one of their outdoor markets to look for something local to ingest. I wasn't going to be a Nixon holed up in the limousine rushing through the *platas* pelted by eggs. I believe native populations can smell the fear. Gorbachev kissed babies on a street in Washington, DC. I can shake a few hands and handle some grapes in Santiago.

Marilyn waited back at the embassy. I was sandwiched in a three-car motorcade. "Stop the car," I ordered. "How do I say, 'How much?'"

The car was already floundering in the market crowd. I like to move through a thick mass of people this way, the ring of security wedging me along, hands disconnected from the faces they belong to reach through to touch me, to try to grab my hands. "Steady, lads," I barked out to the agents.

The squids were huge, draped over clotheslines like parachutes. The shrimps looked like stomachs. Chickens squawked when the vendors held them up to me by their feet. We'd move from the sun to the shade made by awnings of brightly colored blankets and gauzy dresses. I could smell coffee roasting. The potatoes were the size of golf balls and colored like breakfast cereal. Rabbits in wooden cages watched what must have been skinned rabbits skewered on spits turning over charcoal fires. Where we walked, the ground was covered with the skins of smashed vegetables and crushed leaves and tissue wrappers. I slipped on a mango peel.

I pointed at fruit I had never seen before. The crowd that had been drifting along with us hushed to a whisper. The farmer brushed the flies away from melons that looked like pictures of organs in an anatomy book. Stripped, gland-sized berries secreted gummy juices. The apples had thorns and were orange. Another fruit had been split open to show it was choking with sacks of blood red liquid. The flies swarmed around the farmer's hand as he pointed from one bushel to the next. He threw some plums into a sack and waved away the aide who tried to pay him.

"*Gracia*," I said, reaching in for one. I pulled it out and held it up. The crowd cheered. The press took pictures of me eating the plum. I felt like a matador, the crowd cheering me on. The translator said something about water. I told him I didn't want any, that I never drink it. But he had meant that the plum should be washed. It should have been washed before I bit into it. Too late. The bite I took went to the pit. I survived though I was sick later. It didn't matter. I was going to get sick one way or the other. The plum was good. It tasted like a plum.

On the way back to the car, we bumped into a stand filled with carved wood figures of little men. I thought they must be souvenirs like the dolls of baseball or football players you get at the stadiums back home whose bobbing plaster heads are attached to the uniformed bodies by a bouncy spring.

"*¿Cuánto vale?*" I asked the surprised seller. The translator told me what he said.

"Is that the right price?" I asked the translator.

He shrugged. "Seems fair," he said. And I told him to tell the man I'd take one.

I held the figure in my hands, admiring the workmanship. Though crude there was a deftness to the carving, the way the clothes hung on the body. The bright paint seemed festive and foreign. People in the crowd jockeyed around to get a look. The statue was lighter than I imagined, hollow. I shook it and heard something rattle inside. I noticed an unglued seam at the waist. The crowd was shouting at me now.

"What are they saying?" I asked the translator. He told me they were shouting instructions on how it worked. As he said that, I was pulling gently on the doll's head. Just then, the joint below the shirt cracked open and a little flesh-painted pee-pee sprung up. The crowd went wild.

Back then, when I bought the doll, I laughed it off. I told the press it was a gift for my wife. I jerked its head a time or two to show what happened. Everyone in the crowd was smiling and giggling. Security, too, looked back at me over their shoulders to catch a glimpse of the exposition, the flesh-colored splinter tipped with the head of a match.

When I returned to the embassy, I didn't tell Marilyn what the doll did. She found out after listening to the Voice of America on the shortwave. Nothing was mentioned at the state dinner that evening. "Get rid of it" was all she said before turning off the lights and rolling over in bed.

Maybe I should have washed the plum. I was up all night in the bathroom. I brought the doll in there with me. As I sat in the bright tile light, I contemplated the thing. Its enigmatic smile, the way one eye seemed to wink, how its arms and hands and fingers looked like vines grown into the trunk of its body, what did it mean?

Everything I touch transforms into things I cannot begin to understand. I was terrified when I squeezed from my own penis its first drop of semen. I was twelve, taking a bath, soaping myself hard when I felt the shiver. I thought it was the chill in the air of the room, then I saw the little white pill slip out of me. It was soap, I thought. It burned. It had gotten inside. But it wasn't soap. What had I done? Who could I tell? I had hurt myself badly, I thought, and once I thought that, it did not surprise me to then think that I had gotten what I deserved. I have always gotten what I deserved. I washed and washed myself. Years after that, here I was sick again in a strange bathroom in Chile, and a souvenir that didn't have a name regarded me as my insides rearranged themselves spontaneously.

In Chile, I found out later, the ending *-ito* gets glued to every name. It means little, *-ito*. It's affectionate. Little this, little that. And the kind of doll I bought that day in the market is now called *Quayleito* after me.

The guts of the thing are all spread out on my desk. I know now how it works. The springs, the trapdoor, the counterweights, the whole mechanism of the joke. I still don't know its purpose, why it was made. Poor little *Quayleito*. What to do now? My days are empty. Idle hands. Devil's playground.

On *The Little Prince*

The children are out in front selling lemonade to raise money for Jerry's kids. One of them comes running in for more mix. It's a holiday so we all have to shift for ourselves. The old Naval Observatory where we live is near the neighborhood of embassies. A pack of Africans in native dress have surrounded the card table, drinking from the tiny Dixie Cups while the kids are dumping the powdered mix into the picnic jug and wetting it down with the hose. I can see this from the house. Foreigners don't understand why we have a labor day at the end of summer instead of in May. They are all working today, even the Marxists who live down the road. They are heading back to their desks after lunch, killing time at the stand.

I've got the television tuned to the telethon. Crystal Gayle, who is from Wabash, Indiana, is supposed to be on soon. Jerry staggers around the stage. His eyes are crossed, and he's yammering out of the side of his mouth. The French think he is a genius. I hear that all the time. How the French think he is a genius. Personally, I liked him better when he was teamed up with Dean Martin, whose suave manners stood out against his sidekick's clowning. I like the movie where Lewis plays a goofy caddy for Martin, who is a smooth golf pro. The high-pitched whining, bending the clubs, the divots. Martin gets the girl, wins the open. Now, Jerry looks doughy, the sheen on his hair matches the satin stripes on his formal trousers. My God, it's time already to undo the bow tie. What the French say about him has to have gone to his head. He rants at enemies then leers buck-toothed, eyes bulging. He wears aviator glasses that look like copies of the pair the President wears.

French is still the language of diplomacy, I guess. It makes sense since everything they seem to say says the opposite of what should be said. Jerry Lewis is a genius. They use language as a kind of disguise for what they really mean. They praise adults who act like children. Is a genius, Jerry Lewis? I would have studied it in high school, where they made it hard on purpose, all those little *la*'s and *le*'s, to weed out the Z lane kids, who were routed into Spanish. I took Latin because it didn't move around, because it would help me with my English, and because I was going to be a lawyer.

When they were younger, I read to my kids. I took turns when I could and chose the stories with a lot of words and few pictures assuming that, after a while, I would look up and the kids would be asleep, their faces smashed into their pillows, their arms hanging over the sides of the bunk beds. That's the biggest myth, that reading bedtime stories puts kids to sleep. It revs them up, and after I had closed the book, I had to hang around in the dark and answer questions about the strangest things. They always wanted to know if I was there when the story happened and was the story different when I was their age. I'd rock in the rocking chair while they thrashed in their blankets pretending they were characters from a book, that there was something scary in the closet. "Settle down. Settle down." I thought of torts and contracts, the stories of the man who falls down an old dry well, posted but uncovered, on a neighbor's property while he is cutting the lawn as repayment of a previous debt. Who can sue whom? On what grounds? There were ways out of those stories. It ends up being settled. One could walk away, fall asleep.

I could have killed the Little Prince. Reading his story, I felt so guilty for growing up and having no imagination anymore. But one night, I understood that that was the point. I was supposed to feel bad because I no longer had an imagination. The French. This thing they have for innocence. "Go to sleep!" I always wound up screaming. "Pipe down!" I'd storm out of the room, the children whimpering. "Grow up!" I'd yell and yell at them until, one day it seemed, they had done just that, grown up.

I stay away from them now. They have their own lives, their lemonade stands. The Africans must be thirsty. They crowd the table. Somewhere among them are my children refilling their glasses with lemonade that is not lemonade.

Let me try to explain it to myself. Those books never are about what they are supposed to be. Reading transmits a disease that you get through your eyes. A thing like *The Little Prince* gives it to you. You feel worse. You feel like you have lost something you'll never get back. But you never had it and that makes you feel bad too. Therefore: Don't read. Stop now. Don't even crack the book open. In every story there is a dangerous formula hidden in the forest of the letters. It is there already, always.

On *Planet of the Apes*

I was always one of those who hid in the trunk. You paid by the head at the Lincolndale Drive-in off U.S. 30 on the north edge of Fort Wayne. There was an orange A & W shack across the highway from the entrance. We stopped there just as the sun was going down and drank root beers, sitting on the bumpers of somebody's father's car. The parking lot had been oiled, and the heat of the day had squeezed out little blobs of tar breaded with dust. You flashed your lights on and off when you were finished, and a car hop who knew we were from the county and ignored us came over to gather up the mugs. Then three or four of us climbed into the trunk, fitting ourselves together like a puzzle. Two others always rode up front, somebody alone would be suspicious. One of them would drop the lid on us. bouncing it a time or two to make sure it latched.

At first, the dark smelled like rubber, the rubber of the spare tire and someone's sneaker in my face. The car rolled slowly over the packed dirt of the lot, stepped around the ruts, then made a short burst across the highway to join the conga line of cars leading up to the theater gates. It was hot inching our way up to the box office. The trunk was lined with a stadium blanket. Who knows what we were breathing, the mothballs, the exhaust from the idling car. The brakes clinched next to my head. The radio from the cabin was muffled by the seat. I always thought I would almost faint from the lack of oxygen, and then I would. I went light-headed, floating in space, my limbs all pins and needles and the roof of the world pricked by stars.

"Dan O!" They called me Dan O then. They hauled me out of the trunk by the cuffs on my jeans. The car had its nose up, beached on the little hill that aimed it toward the screen. I slumped on the rim of the trunk sniffing the air, looking at the next swell of dirt, a line of cars surfing its crest, moored by the speaker cords to silver posts. It was wrong. I swore I would never do it again. I staggered up out of the trunk, afraid I was turning into some kind of juvenile delinquent. "Book me," I yelled to my friends as they filtered between the cars toward the cinder-brick refreshment stand to buy overpriced burgers and fries with the money we saved sneaking in.

I was telling this to Chuck Heston in the greenroom of the convention. The greenroom was a trailer with no windows parked beneath the scaffolding of the podium. The crowd on the floor above sounded like the wind, and Chuck looked scoured and bronzed. He listened intently, his smile frozen on his face.

"Do you remember where you were from in *Planet of the Apes?*" I asked him.

"From Earth?" he asked without moving his lips.

"That's right," I said. "But where on Earth?" I could see again the inquisitor ape in white robes interrogating the crazed astronaut. This is before we know about the beach with the broken Statue of Liberty buried in the sand. Chuck had been huge on the screen at the drive-in, his head as big and as brilliant as a moon. The screen is now a ruin itself, plywood plates have popped out of its backing, exposing the girders rank with pigeons. The box office is abandoned. The neon has been picked over and scavenged. The high fences are sunk in the weeds.

I saw them all, I told him. *Planet of the Apes. Beneath the Planet of the Apes. Escape from the Planet of the Apes. Conquest of the Planet of the Apes. Battle for the Planet of the Apes.* I saw the first one with my high school friends at the Lincolndale that summer after law school. As a joke they put me in the trunk where I rattled around with the tire iron and the jack.

"I could have been disbarred before I was even barred," I told Chuck. That night at the drive-in, my friends and I sifted through the rows of cars to the playground of swings and seesaws under the screen. I climbed up into the monkey bars and talked with my friends about the future. The huge clock projected above our heads slowly ticked down the time remaining until the movie started.

That night, before I had even seen the movie, I sensed that I was different from the rest, an alien walking among them. I imagined that the amphitheater of parked cars stretching into the dark had come to see me caught inside a cage. I looked out over the expanse of cars. Clouds of dust floating along the lanes were illuminated by the headlights for a moment before they were extinguished. There was the murmur of the speakers, hundreds of repeating messages reverberating in each car. I thought, I'm your man. I'm the one you're looking for.

Chuck hadn't moved. He had stared at me while I talked, his face sagging some as I went on with my reminiscence. Above us the convention crowd howled, a gale force. We would be on soon.

"You," I said, "were from Fort Wayne in the movie." And he looked a little relieved. "The astronaut you played was from Fort Wayne, and the apes took that as another bit of evidence of your hostile intention."

"Oh," he said, "I had forgotten."

"I'm from near there," I said.

I wanted to tell him that back then it had been important that someone like himself had come from that part of the planet even if it was all made up. And now I was here with him waiting for what would happen next.

His head was huge, I remember. As big as the moon. And when the news of his character's nativity seeped into the cockpit of the car, we pounded fists on the padded dash, hooting and whistling. We flashed the car lights and honked the horn until the steering wheel rang. For several minutes, all the cars rocked and flashed, the blaring horns drowning out what was being said on-screen. It seemed at any second these hunks of metal we rode in would rise up and come alive. But they didn't.

On Snipe Hunting

They told me to wait, so I wait. They gave me a burlap sack and pushed me out of the car into the ditch next to a field. I watched the taillights disappear. They told me they would drive the snipes my way. "Wait here." And I do.

Stars are in the sky. I'm in a mint field. The branches of the low bushes brush against my legs, releasing the reeking smell.

I think, suddenly, they are not coming back. Back home, they are waiting for me to figure out they are not coming back. They are thinking of this moment, the one happening now, when I think this thought, that they are not coming back, and then come home on my own.

But, I think, I'll wait. While waiting, I'll think of them waiting for me to return home with the empty burlap sack. They'll think that I haven't thought, yet, that I was left here in the mint field, that I am waiting for them to drive the snipes my way. I'll let them think that.

In the morning, I'll be here, waiting. They will come back looking for me. Dew will have collected on the mint bushes. The stars will be there but will be invisible. And I won't have thought that thought yet, the one they wanted me to think.

The imaginary quarry is still real and still being driven my way.

Seeing Eye

Highlights

This is my office. The clock on the wall is mine. It is in the shape of a black cat. Its tail hangs down. When the tail moves one way with each tick, the cat's eyes move the other way. Usually, I am home by now. This is my salt tank and those are my fish. Those are my couches. Those are my chairs. This table is for the kids and their little chairs. This cigar box full of broken and dull crayons is mine. I am waiting for Mrs. Gustafson to bring Bobby in after football practice so I can fit him with a plastic mouth guard. The Formica tabletop and the waxy scribbles are mine. The stack of magazines is mine. This *Highlights* is mine, and no one has circled the hidden pictures in the Hidden Pictures. I have already found the comb in her bonnet and the bird in the elbow wrinkles of the man. I have yet to find the spoon, the lightbulb, the banana, the pencil, the loaf of bread, the carrot, the ball, the vase, the mitten, the umbrella, the ladder, the iron, and the flashlight. It is a picture of the gingerbread man running away. They hide everyday things in a picture of a fairy tale.

*

I treat kids, mostly, and the roller skaters who wander in from the boardwalk with a chipped tooth from a fall. A bloody incisor in the palm of my hand. I wear a smock with bunnies sometimes or bees. Bright colors, never white. I keep rubber spiders in the light wells to cast shadows overhead. Mobiles twist in the salt breeze. I warm the explorer in my hand. Have three flavors of fluoride from which to choose. I let the children use the hand mirror and look at my teeth. I keep a treasure chest behind the desk filled with plastic dinosaurs, airplanes, and toy soldiers. They bring me their baby teeth. They think I am the tooth fairy. I give them quarters and take the teeth home to Suzy, who says one day she will think of something to do with them. But I find the teeth everywhere, little bits of bone. They will last longer than anything else in the world. The smiles I see here in the chair are all spotty, only temporary. What future do I see in it but braces, orthodontia? All my work gone when the kid's eleven. The baby teeth just hold open a space in the head. Washing out a mouth I tell its owner to rinse and say my name into the funny sink next to the chair.

I have very large hands. My paddles. A hand going through the water has the same amount of surface area whether the fingers are open or closed. They proved that in wind tunnel tests. They were always proving things about the water in the air.

It's all the same. Thicker and thinner.

I could feel the water. Get its feel. I could feel the water splashing into the gutter on the other side of the pool. I could touch the wall before I touched it. I could feel feeling going out of my fingers and spreading through the pool like dye. I could feel the molecules slamming into each other.

But my hands are too big for a dentist. My hands make my patients gag. My fingers can't tell between a premolar and a molar. When I wash my hands with the green soap before I touch a patient, for a second I feel the old feeling. I leave my hands wet. "Open up," I say. Underwater, my hands are two fishes. I watch them through the milky light.

I think Suzy was happiest when she was being saved. The books I did on swimming always had a section on lifesaving. She was always the victim. She has pictures Leifer did. The close-up of the carry where I have pinned her arm behind her. Her other arm is thrown up over my shoulder. Floating dead, her eyes are closed. It is quite tender, actually, the way I am looking down at her, my head cocked to the side, my other arm riding above her breasts. Her makeup perfect even wet. The longer shot as I drag her along. Our bodies all broken into lines by the water I am sculling. My head and her face above the water. Her hair is trailing into the ripples of water. In one, I am carrying her by the chin as I would someone unconscious, but her eyes are open, her eyelashes wet. What was I saying to her? My double-jointed thumb was pulling her mouth down and tight. Then there is the series where I am lifting her out of the pool. Holding her hands on the edge with my own as I climb out. Then bending down to pull her up and over. Pictures are what marriage is all about.

On the boardwalk, the men and women grind by on roller skates. In dry swimsuits, they swim along, arms paddling backward. They float down sidewalks. It is another liquid, a thinner medium. There was a dance once called the swim. They dance it with their eyes closed as they slide past. Antennae grow from their ears, little backpack radios, earplugs, headphones.

"All I want to know is can you do it?" he said from the chair. I'd told him what I was going to do.

"Do what?" I asked.

"You know, man, with the filling. You hear about it."

"Those are accidents," I said, mixing the cement.

"Well, make one happen. I want my molar to pick up KABC. But it doesn't have to be that station. I just thought it would be the easiest. All those watts."

When I was swimming, I couldn't hear a thing. But maybe the ocean. Like the one in the seashell. A sound like metal. You can hear the tide sizzle on the beach. The skaters hiss along. Their eyes closed, their mouths working.

Swimming laps, I would imagine a woman walking on the water a few steps beyond the reach of my stroke. Sometimes, she would trip on a wave and, if she stumbled completely, look at her elbow as if she had scraped it. Sometimes, she would drop pieces of her clothes as she walked. Around her feet would be circles that would expand and disappear when she walked. As I was about to touch the wall, she would step out of the pool as if she were stepping ashore from some boat.

She was not the most interesting thing to think about. So I would begin thinking about the women the other swimmers were thinking about.

*

I am worried about tooth dust. I can see it floating in the air, in the rays of sunlight coming through the window. It is fine and fluid. What will happen after years of breathing it? The mouth is a filthy place. But the dust. I can see it as I walk through it. Feel it eddying around me, closing in behind me. You can write your name in it on the tray; the instruments are grainy with it. It is getting thicker. When I use the high-speed drill, the patient gripping the armrests from the pitch, I can see little puffs of dust from the tooth.

It smells awful.

Worse than burning hair.

No one thought I would make it when I went back to school. I had done nothing for four years between the Olympics. I went up to Canada, but it was the last time I wanted to talk about swimming. The records wouldn't hold. And they kept asking me, "Do you think your records will hold?" I went back home and flew my radio-controlled glider up and down the coast. I would spiral it up and stall it out, tip the nose over and bring it to me like a hunting hawk.

I watched videotapes with Suzy of all the races in Munich, and finally ran out of things to notice. My right elbow bent when it should be extended on the recovery stroke of the two-hundred fly. Suzy would watch Carson, and I would look past the TV at my poster on the wall.

Before a meet you shave down. Some guys do it quietly, others loudly in the shower. The chest, the tops of the feet, the insides of the thighs, the small of the back, even the crotch. Everything is shaved. Doc had boxes of blades and razors.

There was a wall of mirrors, and the guys leaned over the sinks toward them, plucking eyebrows, earlobes, and nostrils, then giving in and shaving the eyebrows.

Some would use Neet. Some would use only a razor. It was like peeling off skin when you did it right. You felt faster, seamless, streamlined. The team from Tennessee shaved their heads and held up their feet to show us the soles with the nicks from where they'd shaved. Well, well. They dared us to touch their scalps. I walked over and poked a finger at someone's bald temple.

"It's in your head," I said.

That is when I started my mustache.

I had a little comb I would use before taking my mark. But I still shaved everything else. I got used to my body that way. When I stopped racing, it was like becoming a man all over again. I grew old in a couple of weeks.

I have dark hair. Sometimes, still, I am surprised by the hand I see working in a mouth. This is my hand. I'll watch Suzy bathing and shaving her legs, raising one out above the soap bubbles like a commercial. She lets me shave the other, knowing how good I am with a razor. Her skin is very soft. When we shower together, I make her lift both arms at the same time, and I shave both her underarms at once.

I cannot remember learning to swim. I like to think that my father threw me in someplace and, as he waited for me to come to the surface, turned to my mother and said, "We have a fish on our hands." If I were a fish I would want to be the kind that has a migrating eye. The eye itself turns the body flat as it comes loose and wanders over the head to the other side of the face. I would think about that while swimming laps. Growing gills, webs, flukes. Evolving backwards. Or maybe the mouth would migrate to the side of the head so I wouldn't have to turn to breathe. Better yet, a hole in the middle of the shoulder blades. No teeth at all.

While I swam, parts came loose and floated free. My nipples slid down my chest. My chin sheered away. My toenails shed like scales. There were fingers in my wake.

I was always thinking of something else. Of one more thing. When I talk to a patient in the chair, before an answer, the mouth is going open, and I can see the tongue still working back in the mouth. The patient makes funny sounds. The teeth, never quite right, float in the gums, washed forward like plastic bottles in the surf.

Suzy got the idea from a television commercial.

It was a floor wax commercial, but in it they machine-gun the glass cockpit of a jet. You can see the white bullets bouncing off. The ingredient that protects the cockpit is in the floor wax. Suzy thought we could make a clear plastic wall out of the same stuff and embed the medals in it. That way you could be sitting in the breakfast area and look out to the living room to watch the television through the clear plastic wall. The medals, she said, would seem to float in the air. I looked into it since I couldn't think of any other way to display them. All the time I was thinking about burglars machine-gunning the wall, the gold suspended in front of them. You could knock on the air in front of you. But they told me the plastic would turn green with age. And what would I do when I moved?

I started swimming every morning when I was five. I turned from the window and picked up my rolled towel to go with my father to the pool before dinner too. Outside my friends were walking away. My mother had turned them away at the door. He is going to the pool. He is going to the pool. Our parents would be on the decks sunning or in the empty stands reading summer books in the middle of winter. It was always summer. And the light was always reflected from below, aqua and turquoise. It was always summer. My hair was always wet or had those furrows the comb left after I combed it wet. And I thought I was lucky I wasn't blond, I mean, so the chlorine wouldn't tint and shine my hair. At college, there were no children. So I would walk off the campus into the neighborhoods or go to the playground and watch the children. There were lots of children in Bloomington. A teacher shooed me away once.

These were the children who had been the test groups for toothpastes. Crest was invented in Bloomington. The unmarked tubes, the new brush, the special tablets that stained the teeth where you missed. All of them brushing together in the school cafeteria after lunch. Those children had been the ones to rush in and say, "Mother, mother, only one cavity!"

We carved teeth in dent school from blocks of clay the size of sugar cubes. When I dream, I dream of two things — teeth that are as large as my head and drowning.

*

When Suzy yawns, I can see the fillings in her back teeth. I'll tell her to hold it and take a look in the light the lamp on the end table puts out. She will go right on watching television. I can see it reflected in her glasses.

"When are you going to file my teeth again?" she asks.

She asks me about striped toothpaste and how they get the stripes in it to come out right.

I do recommend sugarless gum.

If you watch television in the right light you can see yourself watching in the glass. I think television is not so much like an eye as like a mouth. I look and look at it, and I don't know why others see it looking back at them. It's a mouth, all right. When we go out Suzy turns off the television and brushes her hair while looking at the green glass. Her long straight hair begins to float away from her, drawn by the static of the screen. I like to watch her.

Under the water, as I would go into my turn, I would see Doc's face, green, in the window. There was a window in the pool wall so he could watch us underwater. Pushing off, you planted your feet on the glass. He watched us and took our pictures. Around the pool, on the walls, are still pictures of me swimming different strokes — the same strokes stopped at the same point or a series of one stroke instances apart, from all angles. My head coming out of the water as my arms pull on the fly, head-on. What am I looking at? Doc's book was called *The Science of Swimming*. He developed interval training and hypoxic training. He defined the two-beat crawl stoke and the principles of fluid mechanics. He saw Bernoulli's principle in my stroke. I developed my stroke on my own by trial and error. When I came to Indiana as a freshman, Doc asked me how I pulled my hands through a crawl. I told him: a straight-arm pull down the middle line of my body. When I saw the first movies, I saw myself using a zigzag pull with my elbows at ninety degrees. How did I develop such good mechanics when I didn't even know how I swam? Doc said I was a motor genius, and he strapped lights on my fingers and toes that flashed as I swam and made light tracings of my stroke on film.

What I did all at once, swimmers now watch in pieces.

Doc could never get the pieces fine enough. Two pictures that looked identical to me looked years apart to him. They were a slice of a second apart. Like that puzzle in children's magazines where the quintuplets are really twins and three are impostors.

He no longer recognizes me now that I am not in college.

They say one day Doc was surprised by his own picture in a recent team portrait.

I remember the lights on my fingers and toes. I remember the batteries on my back.

There is this bar in Bloomington, Nick's, we would go to after practice in the morning. After telling Doc that we had a class to go to. We'd make our way down Kirkwood against the flow of students heading toward the old campus and their first class of the day. As they would close in behind us we would hear them say, "Swimmers."

Swimmers.

Nobody ever called me by name.

Sitting at the bar, we could look out to the street and the students heading east. Across the street they were building a little mall on the corner of Dunn. Bloomington looked like Indiana then. It probably looks like California now. The stone replaced by redwood, outdoor cafes where the bars with neon signs had been. And roller skaters gliding to school instead of townies leaning into the wind.

The windows at Nick's were painted over with diagonal panes to make it look English. So we saw all this through diamonds.

You drank your beer from old jars.

They sold beer by the pound at Nick's.

She misses the interviews.

Plimpton was the last, four years after all the wins.

We showed him around, ran the tapes and films.

He was interested in what I was going to do now. I told him I was going to be a dentist, and he didn't believe me. I could live on the razor money, he said, sell goggles.

"You could pretend to be a dentist, George," she said, "and come to the office." On the televised interviews she sees now, she watches the wives and girlfriends, how they kiss and hold on to the men who are talking. She likes the ones who never look at the camera but stare up at the men.

I ask my patients questions while we wait for the blocks to take. If their mouths aren't full of cotton, they try to answer. It is hard to talk when half your face is numb. Lips and tongue and jaw are disappearing. I answer the questions for them as they nod their heads.

I keep them in a lockbox at the bank. What can you do with them? I read somewhere in my textbooks about the place in the body that stores gold salts. Like the thyroid and iodine. If you suspect a lesion, you administer some radioactive salts and watch the iodine coat the throat. You need just a little bit of iodine. The same with gold. There is always a bit in the brain. That is where it concentrates, in the thalamus, the seat of emotion. I think about this when I am flushing out a filling, filing it down. There are shavings on the back of the tongue. In the brain, too, a little cavity, a missing piece. If the iodine is not there, you go all puffy. I don't remember what happens if you are deficient of gold. Sad, I guess.

I think of the medals on my chest, pure and heavy. You could bend them and rub off a mark like the crayon color of gold. Not like the metals I mix now — the silver amalgam. Silver expanding, the tin contracting, the copper's strength, and the zinc for flow. All mixed with mercury. Not like gold. Gold is perfect. Gold does not discolor if kept clean. It resists crushing stress. It keeps an edge. It will not fracture.

I think about my medals in the bank vault. Perhaps, if times get tough, I will have them flattened into foil and rolled for the pellets I need.

Could I ever drown? Could I ever forget that much? Is it really like breathing? I am like the cartoon character who has walked over a cliff and hasn't looked down yet.

I watch all the cartoons on Saturday so I can discuss them with my patients. To drown would be the only death that would make sense. The thing that makes you, kills you. The thing that serves you right. The hunting accident for the hunter. But I wonder if I could let myself or if the water wouldn't toss me back. No, it won't be the water that I'll drown in, it will be the swimming.

Someone has colored in Goofus and Gallant. Blue and red faces. *You should hold the gate open for your little brother. You should help him find his shoe.*

I have found all the hidden pictures in the Hidden Pictures and have circled them all with purple Crayola.

Bobby has yet to show up.

This is a nice life — being here, the crayons, the teeth in my pocket, Suzy home.

It's Time

I remember the time each year when my husband cut back the raspberry bushes. I always thought he took too much, afterwards a row of whittled spikes where once a tangled mass of brambles boiled along the fence. He ripped out the dead canes altogether, brittle straws, pruned the branches down to nothing. He dug up the newly rooted tips where last year's growth had bowed over to the ground and took hold, the first long stride into the garden. Every spring, I believed they would never grow back, but in a few weeks, with the days lengthening, the stubby canes streaked with red, budded, shot up overnight.

Does it count as a first word? The other raspberry, the sound my daughter made, her tongue melting into slobber between her lips, stirring before dawn in the tiny bedroom down the hall. It was dark, and the wet blasts helped me navigate, the floors covered with her blocks and toys. Her room was pitch black, the only light the daubs of radium I swiped from the factory outlining the rails and bars of her crib. At night it looked like a bridge lit up, suspended over the varnished surface of a wide, still river. The paint had dripped on the floor, formed a tiny drifting phosphorescent slick. My daughter tottered about. I could see only her shadow, her shape blotting out the dew of pulsing light behind her. She sprayed her one-note greeting. When I picked her up, her tongue rasped next to my ear. I felt her whole body going into the sound, her breath dying down, her spit a mist on my cheek.

"Don't go," my husband had said. "Stay in bed. She's not crying. Ten minutes more. Let her go."

I could see he was looking at the time. I watched the luminous dial of his watch float up off the nightstand. The little wedge the hands made rotated as he fumbled to right the face. From eleven o'clock the time spun to a little past five thirty. "She's up early," I heard him say. The little constellation spiraled back to the table.

Often there were flecks of paint in my hair. He said he could always find me in the dark. He'd kiss me through a cloud of stars. I'd shake my head and the sparks would spill down onto the pillow, sprinkling his face. My fingertips too lit up, stained where I held the brush and the tiny pot. I became distracted with my own caresses, streaks of light tracing his back, neck, hips. Flakes of light caught in the hairs on his chest and eyebrows, blinked on and off as he opened and closed his eyes. Where I kissed him I left welts of throbbing light. His lips grew brighter. It seemed like the fire should die out but it didn't, would only disappear with the dawn in the windows. We could see everything then and still hear our daughter down the hall cooing to herself, inventing a language to call me to her.

This was in Orange right after the war. They used women

at the factory there to paint the clocks. Our hands were steady. We were patient, perfect for the delicate trimming, outlining the numerals with the radium, down to the marks on the sweep face, sketching hairlines on the minute hand. I had sable brushes I rolled on my tongue to hone a point sharp enough to jewel each second. The paint was sweet and thick like a frosting laced with a fruity essence. We'd thin it with our spit. Rich and heavy like the loam in the garden. It was piecework. At the long tables we'd race through the piles of parts, my hands brushing the other hands, reaching in for the next face or stem. The room was noisy. Alvina sang to herself. Blanche reeled off recipes. Marcella clucked. We talked with our eyes crossed over our work, "She had to get married. They went to Havre de Grace by train and were back by noon the next day." We paused after each sentence or verse as we dabbed the brushes to our lips. It was as if our voices came from somewhere else. I'd look away, out the huge windows to the brilliant sky. I can still hear the buzz above the table as something separate from the people there, another kind of radiation in the room that never seemed to burn out. The stories and the songs blend into one ache.

What more is there to tell? Our bones began to break under the slightest pressure — getting out of bed, climbing stairs. Our hair rinsed out of our scalps. Our fingertips turned black and the black spread along the fingers by the first knuckle while the skin held a wet sheen. Our hands were negatives of hands. The brittle black fingernails were etched with bone white.

But this was after so many of those afternoons at the Un-

dark plant with its steady northern light. I remember curs-
ing an eyelash that fluttered onto a face and smeared my
work, how I damned my body for the few pennies I had lost,
the several wasted minutes of work. "I'll race you, Myrna!"
There were many factories in Orange, and their quitting
whistles at the end of the day were all pitched differently.
The white tables emptied, the heaps of silver parts, like
ashes, at each place. Another shift, the night one, would collect the glowing work and ship it somewhere else to be assembled. We ran to the gates, to the streetcars waiting, to the
movies that never stopped running. It was all about time,
this life, and we couldn't see it.

At the trial, not one of us would speak, and the newspapers said how happy we were considering the sentences already imposed. We sat there with our smiles painted over
our lips to hide our teeth. During recess in the ladies, we
powdered over the bruises again. We couldn't blot the lipstick since our skin was so tender. Four clowns in the mirror,
mouths like targets, stared back at us. We couldn't cry. It
would ruin our work. In court, we listened to the evidence
and covered our faces when we laughed at what was being
said. I watched the clerk who recorded everything, his pencil stirring down the page. Sometimes he would be called
upon to read testimony back, and I was taken by the accu-
racy of his words. I remembered the speeches that way. It
seemed right, right down to some of the sounds he noted,
pausing to insert *laughter* or *unintelligible.* I liked these moments best when the words were the only solid things left in
court. The lawyers, the witnesses, the gallery, the jury were

all poised, listening to the clerk. They might have been an audience from another time. The only thing left of us was that cursive string of knots on paper, the one sound in the room.

My daughter loved the fresh raspberries in milk. The white milk coated the scoring between the tiny globes on each berry in the bowl. It looked like the milk drying on her tongue. The berries as they steeped turned the milk pink. She grabbed at the fruit, crushing it into her fist and then sliding the pulp into her mouth.

I haven't been able to speak since soon after the trial, and eating now, even the raspberries so ripe they liquefied when I picked them, is painful. The berries have seeds that shouldn't hurt the way they do. I can't explain this to my husband, who sits reading the newspaper on the other side of the table, his fingers smudged with ink. I make the same sounds now the baby made, little whines and grunts. He's already used to it. I feel I am being whittled away like the nub of the pencil I write this with then sharpen with the paring knife. Why do people lick the lead point? Perhaps it is just a gesture of thought, a habit, hoping that the sound of a voice will rub off.

I'm not afraid. I know this now. It happened this morning when I was picking the berries. The bees were in the late blossoms on the canes above me. The canes trembled, about ready to bow over. Sweat scalded the skin of my arms and neck. The berries hung in clusters everywhere among the thorns and sharp leaves. I have no feeling left in the tops of my fingers, and as I watched my black hand close on each berry, the fruit seemed to leap from the stem into the numb folds on my palm. So little had held the berry in place, a shriveled ball and socket. The berry, a dusty matte red that soaked up the light, bled a little, a pool in my palm. I thought about sucking the raspberry into my mouth, straining it through what was left of my teeth. Instead, I reached out for another berry and then another, dumped them into the pint baskets squashed and ruptured, and rushed them into the house. I found a pencil and a piece of paper to write this down. Each word fell on the page, a burning tongue.

Fidel

My husband, I'll call him David, left me for my best friend. I'll call her Linda. Since then, I have found it difficult to sleep.

I have taken to listening to the radio through the night. The radio is next to the bed, an old floor model filled with tubes that heat up and glow through the joints in the wood frame. My father gave it to me when I left home to live with my husband, I'm calling David. I used it then only as an end table next to the bed. I painted it a gloss red and covered it with house and garden magazines, the bottom one's back cover still sticks to the tacky enamel surface. I live in a city I'll call Fort Wayne.

I listen to a local station, I'll call WOWO. It is the oldest station in town. It's been on the air since the beginning of radio. My father listened to the same station ever since he bought the radio console on time. I have seen the payment schedule. He kept it in the drawer beneath the sad face of the staring dials and the frowning window scaled with AM numbers. He penciled in 37¢ each week after he walked downtown to a store I'll call The Grand Leader to turn over the installment.

One night, when I couldn't sleep, I rolled over in bed and noticed for the first time since I had painted the radio red the two clunky knobs the size and shape of cherry cordials, one to tune and the other the power switch that also controls the volume. Without touching the tuning knob, I turned the radio on, but nothing happened. Nothing happened even after I waited the amount of time I thought it would need to warm up. I turned on the brass table lamp perched atop the pile of wrinkled magazines. I had never plugged in the old radio. I rolled out of bed and onto the floor. Behind the radio was an outlet where the table lamp and the modern clock radio were connected. I had the old radio's plug in hand as I pulled out what I thought would be the plug for the clock radio. It was the plug for the lamp instead. In the dark, I scraped the walls of the bedroom with the prongs of the radio's plug looking for the outlet never thinking to reinsert the plug of the lamp. I had painted the walls a linen white about the same time I had painted the radio red. When I found the outlet the radio lit up inside, green light leaking out of every seam and joint. I was sitting on the floor when WOWO faded in, the station my father listened to years ago when he listened to this radio before I was even born.

The next few weeks I listened through the nights and into the morning. I left the radio on during the day for the cats who I'll call Amber, Silky, and Scooter, as I stumbled off to work. They liked the purring box. In the evenings when I staggered back in I'd find them attached like furry limpets to the shiny skin of the radio. The paint, constantly baked by the glowing tubes, gave off the stink of drying paint again and steeped the bedroom in that hopeful new smell it had when I first moved here with the man I am calling David.

The later it got at night the further back in time WOWO seemed to go with the music it played. After midnight scratchy recordings of big bands were introduced by Listo Fisher, who pretended the broadcast still came from the ballrooms of the Hotel Indiana. Alfonse Bott, Tyrone Denig and the Draft Sisters, the brothers Melvin and Merv LeClair and their orchestras, Smoke Sessions and his Round Sound, the crooner Dick Jergens, who sang with Bernard "Fudge" Royal and his band or with Whitney Pratt's Whirlwinds, and Bliss James singing the old standards. It was as if I had tuned into my father's era, the music slow, unamplified, and breathy. Toward morning the sound was like a syrup with wind instruments scored in octave steps, the brass all muted, the snares sanded, and the bass dripping.

Bob Sievers, who had been the morning farm show host at WOWO for as long as I could remember, came on at five. I had first seen him, though I had heard him for a long time before that, when I was in high school. On television, he was selling prepaid funerals to old people. He didn't look like his voice. And now I heard that voice again thanking Listo Fisher for standing watch at night and then cuing the Red Birds, a local quartet, to sing "Little Red Barn" as he dialed the first of ten Highway Patrol barracks to ask what the night had been like in the state I am calling Indiana.

The sputtering ring of the telephones on the radio sounded swaddled in cotton. It was five in the morning. My head melted into the flannel of the pillow slip. The only sound was the mumble of the connection as a desk sergeant answered in a place called Evansville. He whispered a sleepy monaural hello encased in the heavy Bakelite of an ancient telephone. Bob Sievers, his bass voice lowered a register, identified himself and asked about the weather down there in the southern part of the state. The flat accents of the trooper reported snow had fallen overnight but that the major roads were salted and plowed.

I waited for the next question, lifting my head from the pillow. Bob Sievers's voice dove even lower. "And Sergeant, were there any fatals overnight?" For a second I listened to the snow of static, the voltage of the phone picked up by the sensitive studio microphones. "No, Bob," the trooper answered, "a quiet night." Instantly I would hear the ratchet of the next number being dialed, the drowsy cop, the weather outside Vincennes, then South Bend, Terre Haute, Jasper, then on the toll road in Gary, Indianapolis, Mount Vernon, Monon, and finally Peru. At each post, the search for casualties, the crumbs of accidents. Every now and then someone would have died in a crash. The trooper sketched in the details. The road, its conditions, the stationary objects, the vehicles involved, and the units dispatched, withholding the identities of the deceased until the notification of the next of kin.

There were nights I waited for such notification. I saw my husband behind the wheel of my best friend's car, his face stained by the dash light of the radio. He is listening to WOWO, the big bands of the early morning, when the car begins to pirouette on the parquet of black ice. I know that the radio is still playing, a miracle, after the car buries itself in a ditch of clattering cattails sprouting from the crusted snow. The last thing he hears, the car battery dying, is the quick, muffled dialing of Bob Sievers, his morning round of calls, and the hoarse, routine replies. I think to myself I am still some kind of kin. Those nights, I practiced my responses to the news brought to me by men in blue wool serge huddled on my stoop.

WOWO is a clear channel station, 50,000 watts. At sunset smaller stations on nearby interfering frequencies stop broadcasting and the signal can be picked up as far south as Florida and out west to the Rockies. Just north the iron in the soil damps the power, soaking up the magnetic waves before they spread into Canada. Listening, I felt connected to the truck drivers in Texas and the night auditors on the Outer Banks who called in to Listo Fisher and told him they were listening. Often they would ask, "Where is Fort Wayne?" as if they had tuned in to a strange new part of the planet. Listo Fisher would take requests, explain patiently the physics and the atmospheric quirks that allowed the callers to hear themselves on the radio they were listening to broadcast by a station days of travel away from where they were. "It's a miracle," some yahoo in a swamp would yodel.

One night in the middle of a beguine, a voice came on the radio speaking what I found out later was Spanish. For a moment in my sandbag state, I thought it must be part of the song, a conductor or an announcer turning to a ball-room full of people in a hotel, both the people and the hotel now long turned to dust and the evening just charged mole-cules on magnetic tape, saying to them good night and good-bye. Thank you for the lovely evening. We've been brought to you by United Fruit and now are returning you to your local studios. But the voice kept talking, rising and falling, the *r*'s rolling and the *k*'s clotting together. Every once and again I would recognize a word, its syllables all bit-ten through and the whole thing rounded out by a vowel that seemed endless, howling or whispered.

The telephone rang. It was three in the morning.

"What the hell is that?" my father asked. The words were in both my ears now. I could hear the speech in peaks play-ing on his radio across town, like a range of mountains float-ing above clouds.

"Dad, what are you doing up?"

"Listening to the radio when this blather came over it."

I asked him why he wasn't asleep instead. The radios con-tinued to emit the speech, a rhythm had begun to emerge beneath the words not unlike the beguine it had preempted. Just then there was a huge crash of static. I heard my father say, "What the —" but it wasn't static it was applause, and as it trailed off, I heard the voice say the same phrase over again a few times, starting up again, as the cheering subsided.

"Oh," my father said, "you're awake then."

"Of course, I'm awake," I lied to him. "You woke me up." I asked him again why he was awake.

"I haven't slept in years."

"Well, go to sleep, Dad."

"You go to sleep then."

"I am asleep. I've been asleep," I said.

"What's that crap on the radio?"

"Change the station, Dad. Maybe it's the station."

"But I always listen to WOWO."

I hung up and listened to WOWO. The speech continued for two more hours, punctuated by bursts of applause, the sound then breaking into a chirping chant, steady at first then going out of phase, melting back into itself and the rising hiss of more applause. The voice would be there again. It seemed to plead or joke. It warned, begged. It egged on. It blamed and denied, sniffed its nose. It sneered. It promised. I could hear it tell a story. It explained what it had meant. It revised. It wooed. Toward the morning it grew hoarse. It grew hoarse and dried up. It wound up repeating a word, which seemed too long to me, again and again until that word was picked up by the listeners on the radio, who amplified it into a cloud of noise that this time was static. Then Bob Sievers was on the radio and his theme song was playing.

There are so many secrets in this world. About the time my husband, who I'll call David, and my best friend, who I'll call Linda, started sleeping together, two silver blimps were launched in a swamp south of a city I'll call Miami. They were tethered there to slabs of freshly cured concrete a thousand feet below. I think of those balloons floating there, drifting toward each other, perhaps bumping together finally, and rebounding in excruciating slow motion. The wires connecting them to the ground shored them up, I imagine, so their nuzzling was reigned in, the arc of rotation proscribed. They moved hugely, deliberately, like whales in a tropic bay. Their shadows shifted on the spongy ground below. I am almost asleep, dreaming, when the nodding blimps turn into the slick bodies of my husband and my best friend sliding beneath a skin of sheets, moving as deliberately and as coyly until they are tangled up in each other's embrace and then that zeppelin in New Jersey bursts into flames and melts into itself, the fire spilling from the night sky. There is a voice on the radio crying how horrible, how horrible to see the skeleton of the airship support, for an instant, a white skin of flames.

The curious in south Florida were told that the bobbing balloons were part of a weather experiment, a lie. Their real purpose was to hold aloft a radio antenna aimed at Cuba. It was propaganda radio. The voice I had heard was Castro's, Cuban radio's response, jamming the signal spilling south from the balloons, overflowing on the clear channel all the way north.

For a long time our government denied what was going on and the speeches continued through the night. I bought a Spanish to English dictionary and translated one word I'd catch out of the one thousand perhaps that flashed by, leafing through the book until I found something I thought sounded like what I had heard. He's talking about a ship, I'd think. And he is sitting or he sat once. Overlooking the sea specked with ships. Now there are roosters. Ships, the holds filled with roosters, who crow out the watch. Mothers waiting for the ships, I thought, at the docks, shielding their eyes in the sun, empty baskets balanced on their heads.

WOWO's ratings went up as people stayed awake late into the night to listen to the interruptions, the speeches with the static of applause. And, as if they realized they now had an audience, the programmers in Havana began to salt the broadcast with cuts of Latin music, bossa novas and sambas, anthems and pretty folk songs plucked out on guitars with squeaky strings. Downtown, during the day, I began to see people napping at their desks, sleepwalking to the copying rooms and the coffee machines. More men smoked cigars. High school Spanish classes were assigned to listen to the station at night, meeting at their teachers' houses for slumber parties. So tired, we were infected by our dreams. The days grew warmer. I had been unable to sleep for so long the measured pace of the people around me matched my own endless daily swim through the thick sunlit air. We moved like my cats, lounged and yawned, stared at each other with half-closed eyes.

I listened for Fidel at night. Over time, I counted on him. I translated his rambling monologues in my own dreamy way as he talked about his island with its green unpronounceable trees, the blooming pampas where butterflies from the north nested in the fall, lazy games of catch performed by children in starchy white uniforms chattering in a dialect that predates Columbus. You see, I was ready for someone to talk to me, to explain everything to me. How I looked like a movie star in those sunglasses I wore continually. How fires smell in the cane fields as the sugar caramelizes. I thought I understood romance for once and martyrdom, maybe even revolution. This ropy language, the syrup of its sound, an elixir, was on the air now all the time, crept into my bed each night.

What would my father say? It filled me up, crowding out the mortgaged furniture, the old sad music, the phone calls to the police, and all the names, especially the names I've now forgotten were ever attached to those other frequencies through which I drifted.

Seeing Eye

The kids on the stoops with the dogs are still confused. They tackle the overgrown puppies, tangling themselves in the harnesses and leads as the whining dogs lunge and stumble. Panting. Lots of panting.

"It's the mailman lady," the kids shout. I kind of throw the mail their way with just enough velocity for the postcards to strip away from the bundle, startling the dogs, who soundlessly bark at the spinning envelopes. The kids hang on, use their sweaty faces to spear an animal back, grope for a purchase of fur and skin.

"Letter carrier," I say over my shoulder. Each stride a sidewalk square. The next stoop of the row house has another dog, another kid already mixing it up. The dog's ears are pointing my way. It's stepping all over the kid. And now the whole block of children and animals senses me. "The mailman lady," they howl. The dogs bob and focus, then snap and tumble with the kids, slough them off, cock themselves again. The dogs know. The kids are still confused, don't know what to make of me. Never seen one of me before. The dogs are attentive to ancient messages. The uniform. The territory. I smell just as sweet.

I'm a letter carrier in a town whose main industry is raising dogs. Guide dogs for the blind. Shepherds and retrievers mostly. Big brains and bones. Steady mutts with substantial paws, plodding beasts. Slobberingly loyal. Obedient, of course. Easy to clean. It's still a mystery to me just how the training works. The school is on another route, but I've seen the Quonset huts, the kennels, the field of stripped obstacles at the school. Every year the newspaper does a feature story with a page of pictures of the graduating dogs staring into the calm faces of their new masters. I only know the puppies come here to this bedroom community and are parceled out to families who keep them just like pets. After a while you'll see the dog in the station wagon. A mom is driving, dropping her husband off at the train platform, the kids at school. The dog commutes to work also, comes home for the night, a pillow to a pile of kids in front of the TV.

I run into the older dogs, already on the special lead, as volunteers walk them around the town. There isn't a street where you won't see a couple of pairs plowing the side-walks. The sighted volunteers, waving to each other, nudge their dogs around a corner. They slug their way through a cul-de-sac. At the corners, there are patient instructions. They wait for the light to change and for the scramble bell to sound. The dogs walk through the aisles of the stores down-town. They wait in packs for the special bus that distributes them in the neighborhoods. In fact, the town is overly complicated for its size, presenting to the dogs every possible distraction. Too many cats. Dummy fire hydrants. Revolving doors in the butcher shop. The park has been landscaped in levels. Stairs lead by fountains and reflecting pools. I see the dogs taking cab rides. There is an escalator leading down to a subway station with turnstiles but no trains. They take the elevator back to the surface, where there are flower carts, news kiosks, street singers, three-card monte games, people selling watches spread out on towels, and other volunteers who pretend to be drunk and passed out on benches. Everywhere there are trees. Lots of trees. And people who have signed up to be people today walk their dogs and eat ice cream, read newspapers they then throw in the white wire trash bins scattered everywhere on the avenues. The dogs slog through it all as a car, slow enough to chase, cruises by blowing its horn. I'm part of this too, I know, though the mail I deliver is real. My satchel is strapped to the back of this tricycle cart, and I slalom through the plodding dogs and trainers on the street. The dogs sniff the wheels of the cart. The walkers, for a second tense, lose the strange connection with their animals. My cart speeds up, pulls me along. Up ahead, a wailing fire truck skids around the corner on its way to an imaginary fire.

Along with the letters, we all carry a repellent. It comes in a canister with a pump action like a purse-sized cologne. It is standard issue with the uniform and fits neatly in a leather holster. At Brateman's, the store that carries all the uniforms, I attracted a crowd of men — cops and firefighters, other postal workers, meter readers — as I tried on the new uniforms. The skirt, the shorts, the dusty blue acrylic cardigan still patchless but with stamped buttons. The baseball cap, the pith helmet. I stepped out from the dark dressing room, wire hangers jingling, and the men stopped talking with the clerk who was sucking on pins. They leaned on the glass cases of badges, whistles, and utility belts and watched me look at myself in the mirrors. There were piles of canvas coveralls on the floor, boxes of steel-toed shoes. I tried on a yellow slicker. "How does that feel?" the clerk asked, his mouth full of pins. It felt slick already with sweat. A sheriff's deputy twirled through a stand of string ties. They talked under their breath, examined a handcuff key. A dog and trainer glided through the racks of khaki shirts. I came out in pants that I had rolled up. I have always liked the stripe, that darker shade of blue, and the permanent crease that lets me fold everything back into the shape it started with. The clerk soaped the altered cuffs. In the dressing room, I stood there in the dark, my new clothes folding themselves into neat piles. I listened to the damped voices of the men outside, the dog whining, then yawning, and scratching, panting outside the door. The clerk made out the bill, punched the register. I had clothes for every weather and season, a week of shirts and calf-length socks. Shoes. At last he handed on the key chain and the repellent in its shiny case. "To keep the boys away," he said. I smiled and thanked him, poised over the charge slip ready for the total. I knew it would take at least two trips out and back to the car to load the uniforms.

*

The mural above the postmaster's door in the lobby is being restored to the way it looked when it was painted during the Depression. Scaffolding hides most of it now. The painters move deliberately in the rigging, scooting on their backs or stomachs. It seems to me they are too close to the work. The mural is about the guide dogs. The dogs are marching, leading a parade of blind workers. In the background are ghostly Saint Bernards, Border collies, and bloodhounds, all the working dogs working. The sky rolls with clouds, the rolling hills gesture like a cursive hand. The road they walk is like a signature, too. The painter signed his name in braille, the code of bumps shaded to make it look raised on the flat wall.

In the lobby, the county association for the blind runs the news concession selling candy bars and newspapers, stationery supplies and maps of the city's streets. They let Mabel, who mans the stand, smoke behind the counter. Her dog, a black Lab, curls around the stool, the stiff lead angling upward like a harpoon. Mabel's eyes are a kind of nougat. She never wears glasses. Smoking artlessly, she picks the tobacco off her tongue. It stays on her moist fingers.

My final job of the day is to clear sidewalk boxes outside the station in time to make the last dispatch. She hears me blowing through the lobby with the carton filled mainly with the metered mail in bundles.

"I always know it's you," she says. "You walk on your toes. I can't smell you." She feels her watch on her wrist. "Same time every day, too." I run through the lobby to the back with the mail. On my way out again, I stand by her stand untucking my shirt, letting myself cool down.

After weeks of this routine I say to her without thinking, "You're the only blind person I know." It isn't that she looks at me, of course. The dog on the floor does look up. She pauses and cocks her head.

"You can see, can't you?" She waits for me to answer yes, begins the elaborate ritual of lighting another cigarette. "I don't know too many blind people either. It's not like we run in packs."

The Postal Service has a secret. There is only one key that opens everything. It only makes sense. We can't be walking around with a ring of keys for all we have to open. The banks of boxes in apartment lobbies open at once with the key. The corner collection boxes. The green relay boxes. The padlocks we use. The box at the end of the glass chute between the elevators in the old hotels. Same key. In that way a substitute on the route already has all the keys needed. One key.

I guess it is not much of a secret. If you worked for the post office you know, or if you even thought about it some, you could guess. There it is at the end of that long chain. One key.

They make a big deal about the key at the office. *Do Not Duplicate* is stamped on it twice. I find I am always fingering the key, my hand in the pocket with it as I walk. In cross section it has an **S** shape. It has several deepening grooves and bristles with teeth. I want it not only to open up the boxes of the post office but to turn in every lock, a true skeleton key, opening all the houses on my route. Inside I could arrange the mail further, piles for each family member, on the marble mantel or the little table by the door. As it is, I find myself looking into houses through the mail slot, holding up the brass flap to see the slice of floor and the envelopes and flyers splayed out randomly there. I feel the cool air rush out in the summer. Adjusting my line of sight, I can see walls of framed pictures of grown children who send the postcards I've read from all the islands, the color envelopes thick with pictures of grandkids. Clocks hang on the walls. Coats on racks. And sometimes one of the dogs — I've heard it bark in the back of the house — will come clicking on the linoleum. Huffing around the corner of the entry hall, he is ready to blow the door down from the inside. A snarl and chomp. The flap on the mail slot is already back in place. That's when that black nose points through the door, the nostrils blinking, opening and closing, trying to take in all the smells of me. The fear, the loneliness, my own secret combination of nerves.

Years after the trained dogs leave this city, after they've grown old and blind, their owners bring them back. They trade them in and leave with new dogs.

I'm out at the airport picking up the orange bags of overnight mail when a dog and its owner will come limping across the tarmac. One of the props of the plane they flew in on still revs while the little trucks, run on propane, weave around with baggage and fuel. The dog and the man were the last down the metal stairway, led by an attendant to the terminal. The dog's muzzle is white. Its tongue is out, slipping off to the side of its mouth. There is no color left in the dog's eyes. The dog's almost blind. Its head is down. The shoulders roll. Someone from the school meets them. They wait in the van as the luggage is stowed. I can see the dog's head for a second next to its owner. It shakes itself and collapses beneath the window.

And I sometimes read the notes on the postcards they write home while they are waiting for their new dogs, postcards of the school, a color photograph of a German shepherd at attention rigged out and ready to go. The notes are about Spike or Lady, how the dog took the flight, how the dog is off its food, how the dog seems to remember this place. The writing is little and cramped or big as if magnified. The ink smears on the coated glossy stock of the card. They always love the town, the children on the street. The new dog will take some getting used to. "Buster is making new friends with all the retired pooches." On and on. It's too much to bear. I read these cards and think of losing them someplace or sending them out on the wrong dispatch. They are so sad, I don't want them sent. By the time they make it home, the writer will have returned to his or her life. "Oh that. I'd forgotten I'd sent it. It's just what I told you."

I read these cards in the new white trucks with the right-handed drive and no windows in the back. You have to use the mirrors to see, and everything is distorted.

My family never write but call. My mail is window mail, stamped with the odd denominations of the definitive issues, the transportation series. Each stamp is a special class. Every one's soliciting. The stamps depict all these obsolete forms of movement. Canal boats, milk wagons, stage-coaches, pushcarts, carretas, railroad mail cars, a wheelchair with hand-cranked transmission. Bulk rates, presorted, ZIP-plus-4 discounting, carrier route sorting. When it isn't bills, it is charity, nonprofit dunning. Tandem bicycles, steamships, dogsleds. I read my name through the plastic window on the envelope. I try not to imagine what lists I am on, what those lists say about me. My family call when they have to with important family news. "The mail takes too long to get there," they say. I am too far away to do anything with the news I get. I sign a sympathy note or write a check during the commercials on TV.

I get other calls in the evening or in the morning as I am dressing for work. I answer, and there is silence on the line for a second or two, then the disconnection. This happens often. I shout hello, hello into the static. I can't seem to not answer the telephone. You never know. It could be news. For a while I just picked up the phone without saying a word, listened hard to the silence and then the line going dead. I have to sort my route first thing in the morning. I go to bed early. In the dark the phone rings. I let it ring for a long time. When I answer it, there is that moment of silence and that soft click. Just checking. Just checking. There is nothing to be done. I leave the phone off the hook and wait through the warning alarms of the phone company, the recorded message telling me to replace the phone in its cradle. And then even that gives up.

I have a screened-in porch, and in the summer I sit on the swing as the neighborhood gets dark. With the light out, the kids who come through collecting for newspapers, cookies, band uniforms, birth defects can't see me through the gray mesh. I stop rocking. They rattle the screen door and peer in. Their dogs are circling in the quiet street. Positioning themselves at the foot of the dying oak trees, they crane to look up at the roosting starlings. I let the kids wonder for a bit if I am home, then I go to answer the door. It gets darker. The streetlights come on. The wheezing birds wind down, and the locusts begin to saw. Across the street the lawn sprinklers start up, and the water pools in the street, a syrup on the blacktop. The bug traps sizzle, the blue light breaking into a cloud of sparks. Mosquitoes aren't attracted to the light. I know at least one is on the porch hanging in the still air, sniffing out the heat I'm giving off. Shadows of cats shoot under a parked car. A blind man comes up the street with a new dog. He is talking to the dog. Commands, encouragements, suggestions all below my hearing. I can just make out the gist of things, the cooing and the nicker. A few paces back a trainer from the school walks in the wet grass, skips over the concrete walks. He turns all the way around as he tags along, making sure no one is following.

Once a month the magazines arrive and the clerks will break into a few copies, never from the same address, leaving them scattered on the tables in the break room. After a few days they put the handled magazines in shrink-wrapped bags labeled with a form. Checked explanations for the condition of the enclosed: *Destroyed on conveyor. Fire damaged. Automatic equipment error.* And sometimes someone will go the extra distance, tear a few pages, pour on some liquid smoke.

Customers suspect. They always suspect. I am stopped on the street, asked about the handling codes stamped on the back of the envelope. A *C6* floats in the sky of a sunset on a card from Florida. And *NB* in red tumbles into it. What's this? The bar code embossed beneath the address like stitches closing an incision. "You read the mail, don't you?" I'm told. "I don't have time." I try to explain. "Things get lost. Overlooked," I tell them.

The men at the station like to think they are the first in town to see the pictures in the magazines. One will turn the pages when the other two have said they are through. Their free hands are wrapped around the steaming coffee cups, as their heads float from one cluster of pictures to the other. I'm stuck with the cover girl. I look for the hidden rabbit's head. This time a tattoo. It could be the run in her stocking. The inky smell of the aftershave ads leaks into the room. Business return cards collect on the floor by their feet. They'll forget after a while that I am watching them. Forget to whoop and point. They'll forget to turn the magazine my way, holding it like grade school teachers do when they read to the class. They'll forget, and their eyes will skip and flutter over the pages, the beams crossing and focusing. At last their eyes will be the only movement.

The dogs who don't guide, the pets, the ones too friendly, who can't refrain from jumping up and licking your face, the surly ones broken when they were puppies. We all have our routes. The dogs shuffling through each stop read the streets and hedges and utility poles. These dogs know when something is new. The trash can, the parked car, breaks up the picture in their heads. River pilots and the river. Their noses scour out a new channel, revise the map they carry in their bones. They pull their owners along the cluttered streets. These dogs see through their memory.

I hate to surprise an unleashed dog while he's intent on his rounds. I turn down an alley. A mutt is snapping at a pair of cabbage butterflies. His muzzle draws little circles in the air, tracking the flitting white wings. His eyes are crossed. I can hear his teeth snip. The butterflies are like a whirlwind, scraps of alley paper. Now they tumble around the dog's body, and the dog begins to turn back on his tail, his wagging, until he dives into his own fur on his flanks, collapses and rolls, barks and paws at the insects hovering above his belly. Then, upside down, he sees me watching him. Instantly he is on his feet, pivoting on his nose. His eyes never leave mine. He is growling but backing up. His embarrassment is human, shuffling his feet, clearing his throat. He shrugs his shoulders, scratches his ear, then changes the subject, woofing right at me. I have the repellent out of its case. My arm is straight out, and I am aiming for the eyes. The dog circles, barking, trying to convince the backyards that he knew all along I was there. He takes a few steps closer, the skin on his face tight and his body rigid. It frightens me that I can read him so easily, how the gestures of people inform his every move. But still, I don't know dogs. There is no way for me to enter into his thinking, foolish of me for even thinking, at this moment, that there is a way to explain everything, a way to connect. I think of the spritz of chemical, its sting. I think of the one cord of muscle in my forearm used only when I squeeze the trigger or beat an egg. And just then the dog's eyebrows arch and his jaw relaxes and he starts to pant, a kind of laugh.

Now that the mural in the lobby of the office has been restored, it is much harder to see the dogs, the blind workers. It's as if they bleached the images away. The phantom working dogs have disappeared into the background of sky and clouds now all blended into a hazy yellow soup. Perhaps the paints were cheap during the Depression, unstable out of the tube. Or maybe the restorers didn't know when to quit stripping off age and went under into the rough sketch, the outlines, the patches of mixed paint. The workers seem less uniform but more tubercular. They find their own way. The dogs they hold on to now look hairless. I think it's a shame, but that's just because I knew the mural before. If I'm here long enough, I'll have to get used to it the way it is. I'll forget the old painting, the gray dust the marching kicked up in the picture and the dust itself layered on the painting like shellac.

I almost tell Mabel about the new painting, but I think better of it. Her booth was built in the fifties. It looks like a wrecked spaceship in the marble lobby. Blond wood, goose-necked metal lamps, streamlined steel cash register. The aluminum dashboard candy rack is enamel-plated with the names of extinct brands. I hear the physical plant people talk on break about her concession. What to do with Mabel is the problem. She sits behind the counter touching piles of different things, tightening stacks of bubble gum, riffling town maps. After a while she'll reach down and touch her dog on the floor.

During the Depression drifters would scrawl messages on light poles indicating what houses to touch for lunch. There would be arrows on the sidewalks, a soaped *X* on the brick by the mailbox. So I've heard. Now I just see the kids' games boxed out in colored chalk or maybe a name scraped on the sidewalk with a quartz rock from a gravel drive. I never walk on them and they last.

It's a sad town. The kids are always giving up their dogs. Their mothers give them Popsicles, and they sit quietly together on the porch gliders, pick at the unraveling strands of the wicker furniture.

"Hey, Mailman Lady," one of them says. "My dog left." What can you say?

I say, "I don't know too much about dogs."

The kid says almost at the same time, "He went to help a blind person."

"Well, you've got to be happy about that, right?"

"I guess."

It goes on this way, a cycle of mourning visiting most houses on my route. In the summer, the child, collapsed on the lawn, stares up at the sky. In the winter, he is chewing snow. The kids get new dogs soon, but it is a chronic ache like a stone in my shoes.

On the corner I take out the one key to open a relay box. Inside, the bundles of mail have been delivered to me for the last leg of my route. I try not to think about the messages I am delivering. I file the mail into my cart, stand in a forest of telephone poles, streetlights, fire alarms, police call boxes. The square is crawling with dogs.

The dogs find ways through the crowded streets. They don't stop when children pet them. They ignore each other. They don't see me. They don't bark. They keep going.

Outside Peru

I was cutting the alfalfa with the H when two A-10s skimmed over my head low enough for me to feel the heat from the exhaust.

The H is a tractor. It's red and the first one McCormick streamlined so that the radiator hood looks like a melting ice cube, a charging locomotive, a bullet. The A-10 is an attack aircraft with stubby square wings, a forked tail, and two huge fan-jets stuck on the rear of the fuselage. That day, they were painted five shades of green, a northern European camouflage of pine and lichens. Over the years I've watched the patterns and the colors on the planes mutate — the iridescent splashes of tropic jungles to Near Eastern sand studded with yellow rock, a white tundra splotched with brown. The designs advertise the way trouble grazes around the globe. My cows are always spooked by the flybys. I saw them scatter off the rise in the clover field next to the one I was cutting, angling for the electric fence it took me that morning to string.

The jets are pretty quiet to begin with, and the H chugs a

bit when I use the power takeoff. The breeze I was heading into stripped the sound away. The jets cracked over my head at the same time the air they pushed in front of them slammed against my back. And then the fans whined. The engines reared back like they were hawking spit. I had been a target. The planes are weapons platforms built to kill tanks. They are slow, haul a huge payload of ordnance, can hang over a battlefield like a kite. The pilots wobbled their wings. I could see the control surfaces, the rudders flex, the flaps and the leading edges extended on the blunt wings. They were on the threshold of stalling. Then they broke apart from each other, one going left, the other right, and banked around the cornfield in front of me, meeting up again at the grove of trees near the section road. Without climbing, they tucked in together, the wing of one notched into the waist of the other, nosed over the horizon heading back to Grissom. I let the clutch out again on the tractor, and the sickle mower, a long wing sweeping off to my right, bit into the alfalfa collapsing it into windrows. I nudged the throttle. The engine gulped and caught up with itself. The first cutting, rich, green, and leafy. I settled back to work. Soon, I felt like I was flying myself, sailing at treetop level.

The first calf since I came back to the farm, I named Amelia. With another chance to farm, I was going to do everything right this time. Mom dug out the herd book they kept when I was a boy, the records skidding to a stop around the time all of us kids were in high school. I remember some of those cows. They clouded the barn. Those winters in high school I came home late and stayed up for the milking in the steaming barn. I sat there in the dark, smoking, the radio tuned to WOWO. The cows, heaps in each stanchion, waited for my father to come into the milk house and turn on the vacuum. The herd book has silhouettes of cows, outlines of heads, all scored over with a grid to map the markings. We've always raised Holsteins. The black and white looks best on new grass. I looked at the sketches my mom had made back then. There was Amy with the blob on her shoulder. The crooked man spilling down Apple's flank. As I looked at the old book, I sat down next to the hutch I had just made for the new calves. I flipped through the spiral book to an unmarked silhouette. The new calf's tongue wrapped around the woven fence. She was mostly white except for a spray of black dime-sized spots along the ridge of her right hip and dwindling back down her thigh. Ringing her neck, another chain of black islands aimed toward her eye. There was this ocean of pure milk, white between the black markings. And I stared at her for a long time after charting those few patches. I thought Amelia would be a good name. An *A* since she was Apple's calf. And an *A* for Amelia Earhart, the flyer, lost between archipelagos, at sea.

We had just moved to this farm, I was eight, when the plane buried itself in the big field next to the road. The field was planted to corn that year, and the corn had tasseled. A silver F-86 flamed out on takeoff, the pilot ejected, and the plane arched over and swooped down onto our farm. It disintegrated as it plowed up the field, scorching the ground, flattening the corn, and spraying fragments of the airframe along its path. It came to rest in the ditch looking like an exploded cigar, the engine ashy beneath the peeled aluminum skin. The swath it had cut through the corn was a precise vector pointing back to the base. Disking the field this spring I turned over more pieces from the crash, a bit of fused Plexiglas, part of a shock absorber, the casing of a running light. I threw them in the toolbox of the 20 we use to plow and brought the finds back to the shed, to my dad, who keeps all his scrap. The pile in the back corner looks like a reconstruction of a dinosaur, the whole imagined from a few bits. The wingtip, dented and discolored, resting on the floor far away from the main wreckage of bones, implies the missing wing. Dad has suspended a panel of the vertical stabilizer from the beam of the shed. It twists there, unconnected, could prove the rotation of the earth. The first time we went into Peru after the crash I found a plastic model of the jet at the hobby store. I put it together quickly, then with a soldering iron melted off the wings and canopy, trying to sculpt the ruin in the field. For a long while the whole incident felt heroic. The pilot had chosen our farm to ditch into. I reasoned that from the air our dusty road must have looked like an emergency runway. Later I realized that the pilot hadn't thought twice about it. As he pulled the shield over his face triggering the ejection seat, he believed that no one was down there, his ship would fall into the green uninhabited place on his charts.

Early in the morning, waiting to milk, I've always looked up at the night sky. There are no city lights washing out the view. I watch the falling stars and the meteor showers. I can see a few satellites streak by and below them the puttering airliners. I think to myself, a kind of homing beacon. Here I am, here I am, come and get me.

My father has offered money for a tractor tire someone was using for a sandbox. He scavenges. It's the only way we could farm these eighty acres. We are surrounded by corn this year. To the west and north, the land is owned by an Italian industrialist. To the east and south an insurance company, a thousand acres each. Beyond that, I'm not sure anymore, an incorporated family, rented parcels, more insurance companies. From the air our little grove of trees and the spread of buildings and the strips of grass and small grain stitched together with threads of muddy lanes must look like the center of a dartboard encircled by the alternating eight-row stripes of corn. The bull's-eye would be Wilbur, our bull, lolling in the pen next to the red barn. We can keep this place because my dad never throws anything away and never buys anything new. "You never know," he says, "you never know." Under the old cottonwood trees he has parked the remains of 20s and H's we've cannibalized, and there are all the implements we'll ever need — the manure spreaders, the balers with crates of twine, the Deere two-row planters and the corn picker that fits like fake glasses and a nose on the brow of the tractor. Wagons with bang boards, disks and harrows, a rusting mower conditioner, even a sulky plow, though Dad says he never liked horses. People pay him to haul the stuff away. Now that I am home he has more time to scout around. I do both the milkings. His knees are shot. He walks like he's been dropped from altitude, and his legs look shoved up into his body. They fall straight from his shoulders. We make do with this junk we've got. They can't touch us as long as we don't long for things we don't need. As long as we don't desire to live in the outside world.

I told my mother about the jets zeroing in on me because I knew it would remind her of the summer the red-winged blackbirds buzzed her as she mowed the alleys in her orchard. She wears a baseball hat now while tracing compulsory figures around the apple trees on the Toro. She hates to see my dad go into town because each way has its own junkyard or flea market. Once he came back in a new old pickup hauling a new trailer carrying the old Continental he was driving when he left.

I went to Purdue and majored in ice cream. The food labs I worked in were vast expanses of tooth-colored tile with eruptions of sparkling stainless and nickel chrome appliances spaced about the room. I wore white smocks and paper hats and wrote papers on stabilizing fruit ribbons and fudge swirls. In the gleaming kitchens, I was a long way from the wreckage of our farm. The milk too had been transformed into something else. I thought of ice cream as milk raised up to a pure art form. There was quarried butter fat to dabble on a palette of ingredients — exotic nuts and berries, fragrances shipped to us in plastic tubs, extracts of roots and seedpods, raisins soaked in rum so they wouldn't freeze. I worked in the Union's snack bar too, waiting for pharmacy students to sample all the flavors. They stood there, deep in thought, licking the wooden spoons. I scooped up double scoops for couples who couldn't decide and crossed their cones like they were interviewing each other about the taste. Professors' kids ordered bubble gum, embarrassing their parents, who predicted the disasters just as the first dips cascaded to the floor.

Every spring, back on the farm, the barn swallows build their nests in the same places in the rafters. About the time we turned the cows out after a winter inside the barn, the swallows swooped through the top of the Dutch door, jinking around the post and leveling out just under the mow floor, stirring the cirrus clouds of cobwebs. Then they peel off, flapping their wings once, back out the door. I am scraping the shit into the gutters and plowing it toward the far door to shovel into the spreader. The yard is already mud, the cows mired, moo, their skins twitching and ears flapping. The swallows shoot in and out, daubing the beams with mud and straw. There will be one nest right over the stanchion of Jean, whose black back weathers the summer of droppings from above as if her coat is wearing away.

My parents thought I'd never come home.

If you farm a dairy, you can never get away. That is, if you are milking cows, you have to be on the farm all the time. Milking is twice a day. When I first came back to the farm after quitting school, I tried milking three times a day to increase the yield. Slowly, I broke the herd's habits. The production fell way off. That's to be expected. There was nothing scientific in my methods. I weighed the cans before I poured the milk into the holding tank and marked a piece of scrap paper with the pounds of each. If I had the time between the milkings, I'd draw a line to connect the dots on my rude chart. It looked like a cardiograph. Molly came on in the afternoon, when Clover was falling off. Amy made a sawtooth pattern, like she was singing scales. The vacuum pumps breathed all the time. I was inside the heartbeat of the barn. And I'd hear the cows' big heartbeats through their sides as I rested my head against them, hooking up the claws. Over time, the weight came back up. I could feel it in the cans as I lugged them up the alley. They got used to the new routine, the extra scoop of sweet oats. But I gave it up. I was milking all the time. When I had a chance to sleep, I dreamed of the purple iodine dip I used to disinfect the teats. My whole body was stained. I fell asleep twitching, dreaming about the wet warm muck of the brown paper towels I used to massage the bags to get them to let down.

Now that I am on the farm working, I don't like to ask my dad to do the chores. His knees are bad from the stooping he did all his life. But sometimes I have to get away. I like to take the Continental into Peru. It is the same blue-black topless model that Kennedy was riding in when he was shot. It has the backward-opening suicide doors. I nose into the line of hot rods cruising in downtown Peru and imagine those rear doors popped out, scooping up a bystander off the street into the backseat, surprised but ready to go. Instead, the high school kids always say my car turns the loop into a funeral procession. Watching from the parking lot of the Come N Go, they see the Zapruder film. A creepy car. I am too old for this anyway. I end up buying some cigarettes for my dad and then point the endless hood of the car back to the farm and get home in time to muck out the stalls.

Those nights after I've come back home from those silly trips to town, I hear my parents worrying about me. Their whispers come up to my bedroom through a floor grate there to conduct the heat. I never heard words but sighs that have nothing to do with passion. My mother never changed my room when I went away to school. All the silver model airplanes are still tethered to the light fixture on the ceiling with yellow, rotting string. I never had enough patience to paint them. The glue on my fingers had fogged the clear plastic canopies. The decals are dry and peeling. The planes twist above me, in that rising updraft of worry, like compass needles looking for a true north. On the walls are posters of prize-winning 4-H cows. Behind the planes, they look like a backdrop of clouds, billowing thunderheads, dappled skies. In those pictures, the cows are posed with their front legs resting on little hills that are covered over with turf. They are supposed to look more beautiful elevated slightly like that. But I always think the step-up hill takes away from the picture no matter how artfully it is hidden. I hung up my sketches of the new calves. I ripped them from the herd book. In the shadows, they could be mechanical drawings of camouflaged transport planes. My mother taped up the drawing Annie did when she visited the farm, the butt ends of the herd in a row of stalls at milking time, their pinbones forming a range of snowcapped mountains.

That night after the planes buzzed me in the alfalfa field, I asked my parents if I could go into town. I called them from Peru, from the phone booth in the parking lot of the

Come N Go. Pilots from the base still in their green nylon flight suits, perhaps the ones who flew over me that day, got into the midnight blue van. A National Guard unit on maneuvers. The four of them had Popsicles. I told my mom I thought I'd head on down to Purdue, maybe stay a night.

"Whatever," she said. She wrote down the feeding instructions I gave her for Dad to use. I told her who the vet had treated for mastitis. Her milk would go to the calves and cats.

I said, "I hope this isn't too much trouble." Moths were batting at the light in the booth, so I opened the door to turn it off. I heard the sound of jets taking off over at the base, a sound like ripping cloth.

"You know your father likes to keep his hand in. I'll keep him company." I could see her that night. She would tune the radio to one of those magic stations where the songs have no words and then spread the lime thicker than I do in the alleyway. When I got back it would look like it had snowed inside the barn.

"Say hello to Annie for us," she said.

I brought Annie home to the farm once for a weekend when we were both in school. She was from the Region, in northern Indiana, and had never been on a farm. I went up to Hobart once with her, back then, and she took me to the dunes. We stared at Lake Michigan. I remember it looked like it could be farmed, flat and dusty. We huddled on some riprap and saw the lights of Chicago flare up where the sun set. It is the only body of water I've been to where I couldn't see the shore on the other side, and it scared me. Annie said she felt the same way walking the lanes around the farm. The land just seemed to go on forever.

"When I was a kid my mother told me to not go near the corn," I told her. In the late summer you can get lost in it and panic. It swallows you up.

The weekend she visited the farm, I helped Dad clear out some scrap wood piled next to the barn. We all stood around while he decided what to move where. My mother teased Annie about the rats that would be hiding underneath the lumber.

"Stick your pant legs inside your boots, Annie," she said. "They'll go right up your leg. It looks like a burrow to them."

Dad jiggled a two-by-four. I stood back a ways with a pitchfork. Annie curled over and stuffed her jeans inside her boots neatly. She did this straight-legged like she was stretching before a morning jog, her hair falling over her head. The rat broke out from beneath some barn wood and window frames, parting the dried grass, faking first toward my father, who tried to club it with a stick, then me, then my mother, who was stomping, but then it angled straight toward Annie as if it had heard my mother's prediction. Annie stood perfectly still, her legs pressed together. I saw her shiver. The rat spun around toward me, standing between it and the woodpile. I pulled the fork back above my shoulders aiming at it as it sliced through the grass. I hesitated because I didn't really want to kill it in front of Annie. The rat should have been killed. Its burrow was beneath the grain bin. I just couldn't be gleeful about it. My mother was squealing. I sensed Dad lumbering toward me, thrilled by the chase. Annie stood like a post, as if she had rammed her boots into the ground when she had taken care of her cuffs. Her face was pale and blank. At my feet, I could see how fat the rat was, how sleek and brown, like a bubble of earth was squeezing along under the dead grass. Then, surrounded, the rat stopped dead still. And then, it jumped. It took off straight up, reaching the peak of its climb at my eye level, where we looked at each other. It hung there it seemed for a long time. The rat's little legs were stretched out as if they were wings. It flashed its teeth then ducked its head and dove through my hands. I was twirling the pitchfork like a propeller, trying to find a way to bring the tines or the handle around to defend myself. I yelled. The rat disappeared again in the junk by the barn. We all stood there panting, clouds of dust wound round our faces. Our eyes were fixed on the spot in the air where the rat had hovered between us. I couldn't get Annie to come into focus again. She was a blur a few paces beyond the clear empty space.

That night, Annie and I sat on the couch pretending to watch television. I turned the sound down low so I could hear my dad snoring, the sound drifting through the registers from the room next door. The lights were off. Annie's white shirt turned blue in the flicker of the television. I tugged at her shirt, untucking it from her pants the way she had pulled her pant legs from her boots after the rat had disappeared and we all walked back to the house for dinner. As we kissed, I slid my hand up inside her shirt and covered her left breast. Then, my hands weren't as hard as they were when I lived and worked at home. The only callus left was on my thumb, worn there by the trigger of the ice cream scoop. I rolled the nipple between my fingers and thumb. Even then I couldn't help but think what she was thinking. Just that day she had watched me strip the milk from the cow's tits. I'd wrapped my hand around her hands as she squeezed and pulled on the udders. Self-conscious, I traced a circle around her nipple a few times not to seem abrupt, then ran my hand over her ribs and let it fall on the flair of her hip. She shivered and turned her head away.

"What?' I said.

"Your nails," she said. "That rat."

This all happened a while ago. It has been two years now since I've seen her.

The road to Purdue follows the remains of the old Wabash Canal. In some places the ditch is dry and leafy. In other places, black water has pooled, steeping logs slick with green slime. The towpath bristles with saplings and a ground fog of wild berry canes. Through the sycamores, sometimes, you can see the river itself, green from the tea of rotting leaves. Once, it had been important to hook the Great Lakes up with the Ohio and the Mississippi. The state went broke doing it. To the north is good farmland, a flat table leveled by the glaciers, but along the river the road rolls over the rubble of what they have left behind.

In the low-slung Continental, I was flying. The car leapt off the crests of the rolling hills, then settled again, the mushy shocks lunging with the revving engine. It was still early, though most people were already in bed. The security lamps in the farmyards and small towns draped streaks of light along the long hood like straps of wet paper. In fields beside the road, I saw the hulks of lulling cattle, the debris of herds scattered around like boulders in the glacial till these pastures are built on. The car couldn't go fast enough to escape the gravity of the farm. I thought of my own herd drifting through the clover after Dad had turned them out. All their markings bleed together in the dark so that they become these lunky shadows, blotting out the stars rising behind them. I had raked the alfalfa in the neighboring field into wiggling windrows. The stink of the drying leaves hugs the ground and levels it again with a thick mist, the lightning bugs rising to its surface. For a second, my hands are on the yoke in the cockpit of the matte jet buzzing that field. The cows shimmer in the infrared goggles like hot coals in a pool of oil. The mown field pulses, smoldering with the heat of its own curing. The insects bubble through the haze to sparkle in the air. And I am looking down at myself sitting on the molten tractor, smoking, inhaling the fire of my fingertips, my sweat turning to light. I snapped out of the barrel roll, honked the horn twice, and coasted down the hill into Lafayette.

I got lost in the court of tin shacks where Annie lives, turned around on the rutted, dusty roads in the dark. Somewhere, she rented a half of one of the Quonset huts the university put up during the war and never tore down. Any effort to remove them brings howls of protest from sentimental alumni who remember conceiving their first children in one barrack or another, and the university administration loses interest in renovation. It is cheap housing, a place to store the international students who grow strange grains and vegetables in the empty plots that open up randomly in the court. The spaces mark where a shack has blown up, a yearly occurrence, torched by a malfunctioning gas heater, furnace, or range. The shacks all look alike, though some are decorated with flower boxes rigged by this term's inmate. Bikes nose together in the long grass up against the corrugated siding of the houses. The galvanized metal of the buildings has oxidized over time, so now it has a finish akin to leather, grained and dull. I crept through the rows of shacks looking for the right number.

I had called her too. Her directions were highly detailed but useless to me since I didn't know this place intimately enough to see the details. They were camouflaged by the repetition of forms. I was lost in a neighborhood of Monopoly houses. I only found her because she was sitting on the stoop outside her house watching for the car. When she saw me skittering along the cross street, she stood up and waved her arms over her head and whistled.

"The house is like an oven," she told me. "I was an idiot to cook." She had put on macaroni and cheese when she heard I was coming, and we ate sitting on the front stoop, our bowls balanced on our squeezed together knees. I could feel the heat on my back as it poured out the screen door. There were clouds of bugs shading the streetlights. Every once in a while another car, looking lost, would shuffle down the street dragging the dust behind it.

We talked. I did say hello from my parents. Annie had been working this summer as an illustrator for the veterinary college, rendering organs, muscles, and bones of various domesticated animals. We set our bowls aside, and she brought out several drawings, turning on the porch light as she stepped through the door. She handed me a bone the size of a rolled up Sunday's newspaper.

"A cow's femur," she said. I was never much for the insides of things. I was raised on a farm and should be comfortable with the guts of animals. My father delights in eating the brains and hearts and tongues. I have watched my mother wring the water from kidneys and roll the shiny liver in her hands. I think to myself that I should love, to the point of consuming, the whole animals I tend. Still, something sticks in my throat. When I moved back to the farm, I castrated the first bull calf born. I wanted to raise a steer and slaughter it myself. I named him Orville. He was docile and fat. He did dress out nicely when the time came, but I let the locker do it. I can't get used to it. Sometimes during calving, a cow's uterus will prolapse. I'll find it spreading in the gutter behind her. I can tell myself I know what it is, I know what to do, but when I see guts it's as if my guts are doing the thinking. I stop seeing the animal as a kind of a machine to scrap or fix. Even dairymen need a distance. Maybe especially dairymen.

"Do they still have the cow at the vet school with the window in her side?" I asked her. I would go over there between classes and make myself watch the regurgitating stomachs squeeze and stretch. The cow was alive, chewing her cud. A flap had been cut in her side for studying. I always admired her patience, the way she stood in the special stall letting the technician dab antiseptic around the opening.

"I don't know if it is the same one you saw," Annie said, "but they still have one. The elementary school science classes still are herded in to take a look. They want to not look but can't help themselves."

I could feel my stomach working under my skin, wrapping itself around the stringy elbow noodles, plumbing within plumbing. The bone was in the grass at our feet, weighing down the newsprint sheet with its unfinished sketch. She used a kind of stippling style, all points of ink that clustered into shadow for depth, so that the bone on paper looked worn and smooth as paper, porous as bone, chipped like the china bowls. The dots looked like a chain of volcanic islands on a map of a huge sea tracing the fault hidden under the water.

I told her about my own drawing, the sketches in the herd book. "I wish I had your eye," I told her. Even with the co-ordinate grid, it was still so awkward transferring the markings to paper. "It's just a mess. There are gray smears where I've erased. It looks like they have some kind of mange."

"You like cows a lot though, don't you?" she said then.

"Yeah, I guess I do. I guess I'd have to to do what I am doing."

"But don't you miss," she said, "don't you miss the noise of other people? I remember the farm being so quiet and how you never talked. I never knew what you were thinking."

I sat there on the stoop in the yellow light of the bug bulb thinking about the farm and how I missed the cows, the green fields, and the piles of junk when I was here at school. I thought of the chatter of my own thoughts, how when I work I am always telling myself what I am doing. I am opening the gate now. I am walking into the barnyard. I am driving the cows into the lower field. My boots sinking into the kneaded mud of the yard.

"I love cows too," she said. "The big eyes. The way they just stand there. You look away and then look back and they look like they haven't moved but they have. The arrangement is all different."

"Yeah," I said. "That's true."

"It's like drawing waves in a lake. The calm motion." She shivered. "Spooky after a while."

That night I slept in the front room on a couch that came with the place. The apartment had aired out with the windows and the doors propped open. Annie had tucked in white sheets around the cushions. The vault of the Quonset hut created a kind of organic cavity, and the ribbed walls were papered with her washes of organs and glands. The sink on the dividing wall between the two apartments gurgled when the neighbors came home. I stayed awake, listening to the rattle of their language that seemed pitched just right to start the sheet metal of the building buzzing. They played strange music that ratcheted up and down the walls like a thumbnail on a washboard. Later still, when they had disappeared deeper into their side of the building, I tried to imagine them. I gave them a family life, a routine, classes to take, diplomas they would haul back to the other side of the world, where they would wade in paddies, follow cattle along a packed earth road. And I thought of Annie too, on the other side of the inside wall. I hovered over her bed and watched her slowly rearrange herself, articulating arms, the white rollers breaking along the shore as she stretched a leg beneath the sheet, the tide of her breathing. How she used up every inch of space in her bed, asleep but constantly moving.

Before I left the next day, I wandered over to the Union and had some ice cream, chocolate, in a dish. Students were cutting through the building for a bit of air-conditioning before dashing on to the next classroom. Some would stop and buy a cone, stand and lick the ice cream smooth on all sides, manageable, before they rushed off. The Union is camouflaged with Tudor beams of darkly stained wood and stuccoed walls. I hadn't remembered it being this much like a barn. Lumps of students sleeping in leather club chairs or single ones swaying in study carrels, reading, tucked in nooks behind squat square columns. I knew where the milk had come from to make the ice cream, but no longer remembered the origin of chocolate. South America? Peru? The other Peru? Which was the more exotic ingredient, the stranger place?

I drifted over to the library across the street from the Union. It was hot out, and I promised myself I would hang around the campus till the sun went down, then drive back home in the dark. When I was a student, I liked to look at the special collections the library had on flyers and airplanes. Neil Armstrong went to Purdue. A lot of astronauts did. I don't know why. And the plane Amelia Earhart disappeared in was owned partly by the school. At the time she was a professor of aviation or something. There are pictures of her in her flying jacket and slacks having tea with women students. They crowd around her. I love the pictures of her posed with the silver Electra, poring over maps of the world in this very room of the library. The room seemed even more crowded now with trophy cases, photos, charts, and models. There were navigation instruments and facsimiles of her notes and letters. I looked at a milky white scarf arranged as if casually flung along the black velvet shelf encased in glass.

A librarian was typing labels in an office off the main room. Behind her there was a picture of the librarian receiving the school flag from two astronauts. It looked like the ceremony was taking place during the halftime of a basketball game.

"The flag had just come back from the moon," she told me. "I have it here someplace."

I told her I was interested in Amelia Earhart's time at Purdue. I like to think of her circling above the countryside, perhaps looking down on our farm. It isn't that far away. I sat down at a polished table where she brought me an album stuffed with local news clippings, brittle and yellowed, pasted to the black pages.

"They found her, you know," the librarian said. "They think they found her."

"What?" I said.

"Or what remains of her," she said, "on an island in the middle of nowhere. They found a navigator's aluminum case washed up on an atoll. They're going back this summer to find the plane and what's left of the bones. They came here to look at the photos, to see if they could see that same case in one of the pictures."

That night, I drove home with the top down on the Continental. I climbed and stalled and dove through the hills along the Wabash. The metal skin of the car was the color of the night and the road. I let myself lose track of what was what. All that was left was this little ellipse of upholstered light I sat in, gliding through space, adhering to the twisting white rails emitted by the low beams. Annie had sent her love to my parents, and I thought of it, her love, as a slick, gleaming, and, as yet, undocumented organ I was keeping right here in my silver navigator's case. It had been easy, the librarian had said, to find the little island in the middle of the Pacific once the searchers guessed the slight miscalculation that led Amelia Earhart off her course. They followed the string of physics into the sea. As I drove, my cows drifted from the light of the barn, sifting through the gates and alleys to the highest part of the farm, the rise in the clover field, there to catch the slight stirring breeze. In their own way, they tell themselves what comes next. Wait, they say, and the next moment they say wait again. Me, I wanted right then to get lost on my way home in the middle of Indiana, but I knew, deep in my heart, that that was next to impossible.

Turning the *Constellation*

I try to see the stars through the rigging and the old reefed sails. The lights from Pratt Street bounce off the edge of the still water in the Inner Harbor. Beyond the pavilions of Harbor Place, downtown Baltimore steps back in terraced, floodlit cliffs with outcroppings of red neon logos. The light seems to steam off the buildings.

The soft pools of light from the paper Japanese lanterns strung above the deck spot the polished fir. Couples shuffle around the masts and hatches, keeping time with the brushed snare of the combo set up in the stern. Once, boys they called the powder monkeys smothered this deck with sand right before a battle so the bare feet of the crew could gain a purchase on the planking. It mentions this in the souvenir program of the evening. The old wood frigate must be turned each year so that she'll last longer as a static display. They've made the maintenance into an event. Half of Baltimore is on the docks to see us shove off. We party on the deck while the crew casts away the lines. The tugs nose up against the sides of the ship. The launches taxi back and forth over the black water.

In the still water of the Inner Harbor, I think I see a sky full of stars. Then I remember that the bay is saltier this year, and the sea nettles and the Portuguese man-of-wars have been drawn into the estuary. Tonight, they give off their own phosphorescent light in a frequency below the sodium vapors coating the downtown. Shading my eyes, I can almost see into that sky of water as those stars wheel with us and turn on the high tide.

They shipped Nelson's body home from Trafalgar in a cask of brandy. You say, "Byron's too!" I wonder how it worked. Were the barrels big enough for the bodies to float? Or were they doubled over, embryos again, ingeniously folded as grape leaves in a jar? Our brandy sloshes around the sides of the snifters. We glide by the dark hulks of the submarine and the lightship at their slips. More museum ships. The water churns white from the bite of the tugs' screws. The pilot boats sweep the deck with floodlight. The liquor catches and then shatters it. Bright jewels bob above your cupped hand.

It is close below on the gun deck. A few naked bulbs patch together some light. In the shadows the sleeping hammocks strung between the beams look like ancient cobwebs. The rose odor of gasoline drifts up from a few decks below, where the generators rasp away, and beneath that the bilge pumps pant. We dance a step or two. We're not supposed to be here, but the empty deck looks like an old ballroom. Only the masts break up the space. Above our heads the upright bass sends a beat into the timber, and the whole ship seems to resonate. We are dancing in the guts of a guitar, the sound, all around us. "What a fine coffin," you say.

A soggy breeze laps at us as we look out of an open gun port. We're closing on the Domino Sugars sign, which, from this angle, looks like a city burning on a hill. Sliding my hand along the lip of the loop, I lodge a splinter in my finger. "Some sailor you are," you say and hold my hand to your face. Your eyes cross, and you catch the tip of your tongue in your teeth. "It will wait until we get home," you say. "I'll have to use a needle." The light from the burning sugar sign polishes the dollop of blood you've squeezed from the wound.

I am in retirement from retirement. I hope to forget what I did at Social Security all those years. I wrote letters. I listened to stories, a fiduciary chandler outfitting final voyages. I tended all those sputtering candles, a bank of votive lights. I reassigned the numbers when the checks came back unsigned. The computers there were as big as ships. And you teach composition to midshipmen down the bay. The literature of salt and Odysseus returning home each spring term. I imagine you looking out your office window, watching the sculls cut through the Severn and, out farther, the little sunfish stagger around a buoy in yet another race. This is our shipboard romance, not very important people among the other invited guests: the crooked politicians, the tarnished Navy brass, the Rouse Company execs and the doctors from Hopkins Hospital, the flush philanthropists, the car salesmen and restaurateurs, *Evening Magazine,* the odd Oriole signing starched white shirtfronts.

Imagine the wounds from the wood when it splintered in those broadsides. The double shot leaving the muzzle was slow enough to see, the trajectory as flat as a throw to the plate. The wood, elastic, shrugged off the balls but not before they chewed off a slice of pine or pulverized the oak, turning it into a kind of atmosphere the gun crews breathed in with the black ignited powder. You say this as you dig into my wounded finger with your nails. All this wood. England cut down every oak to smash them up at sea. You read about the endless voyages of wooden ships bound in books so thick they could stop a bullet. And there was the pulp my department floated on: the tractor-fed girdle of paper run through the printers, the newsprint barked with chips, and the legal pads laced with a dust of fibers as fine as the motes that float in the fluid inside your eyes.

I bought you a star. I used my Visa when the call came during dinner from a boiler room scam in Ohio. Thirty-five bucks. They sent a certificate and sky charts with the star, a speck of puny magnitude, highlighted with a yellow marker. I thought once out in the harbor away from the lights of the city we'd be able to see it ground beneath the heel of a twin. The charts are in my pocket. The zodiac all stitched together. I never was any good at seeing the tacked up hides of the old stories in the night sky, took other people's word that they exist at all. Even the single drip of the North Star can't lead me back to the Dipper. Or is it the jewel in the handle's crook? I've always liked the shooting stars, the showers of sparks struck off the dome of heaven I can only catch in the corner of my eye. By the time I turn to look, the streak's extinguished, so I'm not even sure it was there, a kind of memo that's sent to the shredder. Look, there's one now.

There. A red navigation light strobes on top of the old shot tower. The rest of the red brick is black in the night. It blots out the skyline behind it, a gap in a grin. We'll have time now for all this history. I can see us climbing the spiral staircase like smoke in a chimney, up to the platform where they dropped the boiling lead, letting it fall into the vat of water six stories below, the hot rain freezing into hail. The cove and creek bottoms of the Eastern Shore are silted with shot that falls back to earth. The ducks scoop up the pellets for their gizzards. The lead that missed them on the wing kills them finally. And we'll go next door to the Flag House, where the Star-Spangled Banner was pieced together. The ensign, big enough to wrap the little row house, clouded the rooms with bunting. The woman picked through the cloth as it crept over her lap. One white star dwarfed the whole front parlor. We'll have to see it, the way the flag was folded into the house, another miracle of packing, like the whole sky tucked into my pocket or those bodies steeping in their kegs.

"What are you doing down here?" the Marine says. He jogs toward us, skipping over cables. He wears a bowler hat and a short green jacket. We're not supposed to be below but up above with the party. We hear them hailing the little sailboats and inboards swarming alongside. The branch has widened here, and the channel is newly dredged. The boats wallow in the wake of the tugs. We follow the volunteer aft along the gun deck. He's from Highlandtown, a jarhead in Korea. He draws a pension from Bethlehem. Now he mends his uniforms for the summer of reenactments. "The Civil War's the war," he says. "The encampment down at Manassas is near as big as the battle was." He slips in and out of character. There is so much to save now, he thinks. He's part of the industry of preservation. We watch you climb the open ladder up into the night. I remember you climbing back into the upper berth of the Pullman we took to Chicago. That silly ladder hooked into the loft. With the overhead lights off, we had slid the shade up and left on the one pale blue light near my bed. There was no way for you to be graceful, each rung forced you to splay your knees apart. The train rocked. You threw your body into the bed above me. Below, my vantage all screwy, you foreshortened, and your toes turned white on the last step. You floated into a heaven of webbed luggage while the porter felt for our shoes in the locker by the door. I don't tell the Marine this, but follow you up to the main deck, my face in your skirts.

The traffic helicopters from the television stations seem to be caught in the yards of the foremost tops. The pennants there begin to stir as if the light from the helicopters' swiveling spots drove the air. The choppers pivot on the beams shining down. Their long, tapering tails stir around. Miss Ethel Ennis is singing a jazzed up version of the national anthem with the fort just off the starboard, and the guests can't make up their minds if this rendition counts enough to settle down and salute. There is champagne with cold soft crab sandwiches. The Governor takes a turn at the helm, spinning the unconnected wheel after a brief toast. The cameras in the helicopters never stop moving. The lights on the deck spin beneath them. Watching the news tomorrow, we'll be hungover enough to forget how to see, how to make the cameras pan. Instead the ship will roll and yaw, the masts raking at us dodging the streams of light.

Most of the dignitaries have been piped off the ship, sailing away in a fleet of speedboats toward Fells Point. We've talked the crew into letting us stow away to wait with them for the morning tide and the ride back to port. The band is packing up on the quarterdeck. The bass player, in shadow, wrestles the body of his instrument into the case. We watch the caterers break down the tables, snitch swipes of crab salad on crackers before it turns in the heat. The *Constellation* will ride the night out here in the bay with its skeleton crew. She'll head in tomorrow with the tide, to her berth, her bowsprit now poking in toward the upper windows of the shopping mall she poses next to. She'll weather more evenly, the Marine had said, the weather hitting her like a slower broadside. We watch the divers in the dark water. Their heads tip forward. They disappear together. They are inspecting the hull. Blind, they feel along the keel and try to imagine what has cemented itself to the old copper sheets below the waterline. We wait for the divers to surface, their black rubber suits shedding the light of the full moon, an oily sheen. We try to guess where they'll appear in the black water, but they never do.

I say, "A friend of mine died, and he had always wanted to be buried from his boat, wrapped in a sail and tipped overboard into the bay. His will charged a group of us with handling the details. So we looked into it. We thought it would be simple, a few pieces of paper. But the state of Maryland requires a crypt with the coffin, a big concrete vault that would have sunk his little boat if we even could have gotten it onboard. We thought of hiring a dredge with enough room for the casket and its casket, and we realized the estate would be eaten up by the costs. The body still had to be embalmed, permits obtained for dumping chemicals into the water. So, on a night like this, we wrapped the body up in canvas and lead sinkers and sailed out to the ship channel, where the tankers rode at anchor as they waited for a chance to dock, and dropped him in the deepest water we could find inside the Bay Bridge. We buried the empty casket in a crypt in a cemetery on Belair Road."

You say, "You are such a liar. Who was this friend who died? Who were the friends who helped you? Did you buy off the undertaker to look the other way when you loaded the body into the trunk of your car? Wouldn't the body be tonged up by some startled waterman sooner or later? I know you too well. I've heard you tell the story at too many barbecues with a glass of champagne you use as a model of the little ketch heeling in the bay and in the lobbies of funeral homes where your real dead friends are being shown. After you've taken a glance at the body, you say, 'A ghastly business, this viewing.' And in some versions, it isn't even you at the tiller on that moonlit night. Another friend of yours has done the deed. He has told you the story at a wake of a mutual buddy as you stand by the body. A cold nose, like a luffing sail, just shows above the open hatch of the casket with its spray of taffeta. But I love the story because it is the story you tell over and over. It's a spell, another form with carbons, to ward off the bureaucracy of time. It is a bribe to get around the rules. You've lived through another night. You've buried your stand-in at sea. You whisper the story in the parlors of funeral homes while, kneeling near the body in the next room, the old women race through the rosary, the sorrowful and the joyful mysteries. Listen, the last stitch the sailmaker made when he made the shroud at sea went through the stiff's nose. A detail from a book I read. Its pages sewn together too, that ancient repetitive gesture of time and story-telling."

The moon is so fat it can't lift itself much higher than the Key Bridge, a fresh suture in the sky. Its mealy face is ready to blister like paint on a balloon. The old skin will slough off. This has been going on a long time, this moon turning old. There is enough light to wash out the stars after all. Mars, always heading toward us, follows the moon toward

Virginia. The very old light from the biggest stars happens to reach our eyes at this moment. We are stretched out on the deck looking up through the nets in the rigging. The live oak in her frame is decaying in measurable amounts, an ambient rot. The souvenir program says the wood is original, America's secret weapon. It gets harder in brine. They couldn't work it two hundred years ago. When they pulled it from the swamps and bogs of the Carolinas, their saws and chisels blunted. My tux is rented, has its own history of sweat. Along my back, I feel the splinters of radiation prickle my body with its own stores of carbon, its rings of skin. I say that sliver of wood in my hand will fester, the infection will streak toward my heart. "Baby," you say, "it will work its way out."

The telescope they sent up into space was supposed to prove there are other planets around the suns we see as stars. It is floating above us now, a blind hulk, its perfect mirror ground to the wrong formula. All that preserved junk of fabricated senses spirals around us as we spin. I would have aimed the thing back down at us, a civil spy satellite, with a bank of scientists interpreting the semaphore of, say, two human bodies in a bed, reading them like letters on a page.

Getting ready for the day, the crew is hoisting signal flags, pennants, ensigns, and Perry's battle flag quoting the dying Lawrence on the Chesapeake. There are no poems for this ship. Who remembers the quasi-war with France, Truxtun, the hostages held by the beys of the Middle East? Here we are, drowsy, on watch on the poop of an old ship. The moon has gone, and the breeze has freshened, blowing the swamp away toward the Eastern Shore. There the stars are finally opening their eyes, and nobody can see us.

The fireboats have come out to greet our return voyage, and the light is breaking up in the arching water of their cannons. The mist on the water smolders. The sun behind us chisels from the haze the row houses climbing Broadway. Everything is new or ancient. We can just see the piers crowded with people. The cranes and the gantries of the city's construction could be the rigging of tall ships. I am getting too old for this. My archaic joints are ungreased wood, creaking like the frigate, her spars rattling in the headway she is making. But I unfold myself and stand into the wind. On the wind is the smell of Baltimore, the spices from the factories on Light Street that survive near the shopping malls, offices, and hotels. The spices mask the frightening stench of sluggish water, suggest the Orient, a new port opening to trade. The dried fruits and crushed leaves of another season preserve us all, home after a long passage, anoint our memories at the same time they come flooding back before us.